THE JUDGEMENT GAME

CHARALEE GRAYDON

ISBN-10: 1481945912
EAN-13: 9781481945912
Library of Congress Control Number: 2013900668
CreateSpace Independent Publishing Platform
North Charleston, South Carolina

The Judgement Game is a thought-provoking book about today's justice system. If someone has always thought of punishment in strictly black-and-white terms—one punishment fits all—he may not after he is asked to judge the cases found in this manuscript.

The Editor

WARNING – Not suitable for children; contains adult themes; violence, explicit sex and coarse language.

AUTHOR BACKGROUND

Charalee Graydon was born in Alberta, Canada. She holds degrees in arts and law. Following receipt of a Rhodes scholarship in 1982, Charalee pursued post-graduate legal studies in Oxford, England. She held academic positions in England, New Zealand, and Canada and practised law in Canada. She developed programmes for students, judges and the public and published academic works on legal issues and crime and punishment. She created and taught a course at the University of Alberta on sentencing and has given radio and television interviews on this topic. She holds a diploma in Freelance and Feature Writing from the London School of Journalism and is a journalist for an on-line photography agency.

MESSAGE FROM THE AUTHOR

The Judgement Game asks you to play a game. This work of fiction provides a series of vignettes to allow you to take part in the criminal and civil justice systems of your country, Torcia. This is an interactive book about ideas and decision-making.

The game asks for your comments about the offences and offenders. It seeks your ideas about responses and penalties. You are self-taught, and your knowledge and opinions are respected. You are providing new ideas for Torcia´s justice system. There are no right and wrong answers in the game. *The Judgement Game* is about returning justice to the people.

The Judgement Game is the modern literature of crime and punishment.

The Judgement Game   www.charleeg.com

charaleeg.wordpress.com

ACKNOWLEDGEMENTS

To my friend Jose Luis Arroyo Vallejo, Christine Coirault author from England who reviewed proofs of *The Judgement Game* and provided valuable advice, Kamal of Photofade.com for word press and website design, and Dani Mandrágora for photography, Mhamed Riouch for IT assistance, Martine Vié for wisdom and common sense, my family and friends around the world, the prison guard who wrote poetry about a quest for freedom and the deity that has guided and continues to guide me.

INTRODUCTION

• • •

You live in Torcia. You will read vignettes about criminal and civil offences in the homes, streets, and prisons of your country. *The Judgement Game* seeks your ideas about the problems that have occurred and the responses and punishment to be imposed on offenders.

The country of Torcia is a society defined by sex, greed, and addictive behaviour. Traditional systems of crime and punishment don't seem to be working. *The Judgement Game* invites you to find out what has gone wrong and what can be done about it.

You are playing a game that has been played for centuries. You need only use your experience and decision-making power to help Torcia find answers to its problems.

The type of punishment Torcia will use and why is your decision.

THIS IS YOUR JOURNEY:
A QUEST FOR THE SELF WITHIN
THE MYSTERY OF CONSCIOUSNESS

CHAPTER 1:
DANCING WITH A LEOPARD—
CASES OF DOMESTIC ABUSE

• • •

YOU ARE THE AUDIENCE

My name is Fiona. I want to tell you about life with my boyfriend Tom.

It was a cold November evening. I had come home from work with Greg, a colleague from my office, who wanted to borrow a book I had recommended he read. Tom said hello when we came in but seemed upset about something. It was only later when we were getting ready for dinner that he told me what was wrong. He accused me of having an affair with Greg. I denied I was having an affair, but I could not reason with Tom.

With aggression in his voice, he said, "I saw the way he looked at you. I know that you are having an affair with him. Don't try to deny it."

When I laughed, Tom lost his temper. "You bitch," he shouted. "Don't laugh at me. I know your sort." I knew that Tom was sensitive and jealous of my interaction with other men. He was abandoned by his father at the age of five and had been raised by an abusive mother who lived with different men while Tom was growing up.

I tried to make light of the situation by saying that Greg was too chubby for my liking. I walked behind Tom to stroke his neck.

He grabbed me by the arm and said in a menacing voice, "I know what you want from me." He pulled me down the hall to the bedroom, where he threw me on the bed. I was crying and struggling to get up.

"You're a bloody whore," he screamed at me.

I was frightened but tried to lie still so as not to antagonise him. I didn't know why he was acting so crazy. He took one of the pillows and held it over my face. I couldn't breathe. My only thought was, this is the end. He is going to smother me.

For some reason he backed away from me. Just long enough for me to jump up and run. Why did he allow me to try to escape? Perhaps it was a game to tempt me with freedom and then follow me like a hunted animal. He caught me as I was running out the door to the street. He dragged me back to the house and started shaking me and banging my head against the wall. His hold on my throat was choking me. I couldn't endure the pain. I slipped into a semi-conscious state. I knew I no longer had control over his actions or what he would ultimately do with my life.

I slipped from the reality of his anger, from his hatred of something far from me, to the serenity of nothingness and the calm of black.

When I returned to awareness, I heard Tom say, "I should kill you. You shouldn't have brought him home with you."

I heard a knock at the door. I struggled to get up. Tom was silent. Why did he let me get up? I stumbled to the door.

When I opened the door, two police officers stood there. Someone must have called the police. The officer said he had received a complaint that someone at this address had been screaming. He asked if everything was OK. All I could say was, "Please help me."

He didn't ask me more. Calmly and professionally, I was taken out of the house. I tried not to cry. The officer, who was clearly no stranger to cases of domestic violence, said he would take me to the hospital. I saw the other officer go into the house to speak to Tom.

At the hospital, I was checked for recognisable affects of abuse. They looked for broken bones, fractures and measurable skull injuries. I was told I was fine and was released. The police officer told me Tom would not be at the house when I got home. He had been arrested and charged with assaulting me. The officer asked me if Tom had ever hit me before. My response, "too many times." I told him I'd never called the police because I thought we could work things out.

I learnt that Tom was sent to jail. The police said he entered a guilty plea and was sentenced to twenty-four months incarceration. I did not have to go to Court. It was over quickly and Tom went to jail. I went on with my life as if nothing had happened. I knew, however, that it was not over. I didn't know what to do. I thought about moving, but knew he would find me.

Sure enough, when Tom was released from jail, he came back to my house. It was a Sunday and I was at home. He rang the doorbell and said he would like to come in to talk to me. He told me he had just been released from jail and had nowhere to go. He begged me to forgive him and to take him back. He told me he had changed. He said he had taken courses in jail and learnt how to deal with his problems. He said his course instructor told him he had an attachment disorder and had provided ways for him to overcome his lack of trust and fits of jealousy. Tom said that he told me this in order to help me feel safe.

I didn't know what to do, but I knew I couldn't let him come back to live with me. I told him I couldn't take him back.

Tom didn't seem to care what I said. When I said I would not take him back, his manner changed completely. He told me I had better let him in and give him a second chance. He said he had come back because he loved me and would make things right. I didn't know what to do. I was frightened by the way that he was speaking. When he reached over to hold my arm, I felt the strength of his grip and knew there was no arguing with him. He was coming back to the house.

I didn't contact the police or tell anyone he was back. I thought it best to wait until he tired of me. I knew there had been other women in his life before me and thought that if I remained distant he would move on.

It wasn't long before I noticed he was spending a lot of time out of the house and coming home late at night. He spoke about a man he met in jail who had also been released. He mentioned that the man was married and lived in the city with his family. I thought it a good thing for Tom to have friends. Tom never invited the man to the house but, from Tom's comments, I knew they were spending time together at bars. I never heard more about the man's wife or family. Tom started coming home later and later every night.

I was working both in and out of the city and did not have time to worry about what Tom did each day. He told me he was looking for a permanent job but had not been able to find anything. He seemed to have pocket money, so he must have found some work that paid him on the side. He knew, of course, that I was looking after the mortgage, electricity, telephone, and groceries. I was happy to do that until he asked me to do more.

Tom started bugging me about helping him find a permanent job. He said he wanted to buy a new car to use for jobs he had been applying for. He said I was stupid if I didn't help him because if he had a better job, he would be able to help with our expenses. He asked me to co-sign a loan so he could buy a car, and when I refused, he became angry and stormed out of the house.

He was gone for a week and I prayed he had decided to leave me. I still did not contact the police or tell anyone that he was back in my life. I just closed my eyes and hoped he would not return.

He came back after a week. He never said where he had been, and I didn't ask. Tom was back in the house but did not want to speak to me. I could see he was still upset about the loan. When he spoke to me, it was to criticise something I had done.

I knew things would get worse and I had better make plans to get away from the relationship for my own safety. The only thing I told Tom was that I had to go out of town on a business trip the following week. My work as a sales representative for an insurance firm often required me to travel, and Tom did not seem to take notice that this was any different from my ordinary activities. He didn't know that I would take steps to cancel the heating, electricity, and the telephone before I left. Everything was in my name, and I wouldn't have any problem cancelling the services. I only needed to endure one more week of Tom's behaviour and try not to alert him to what I was planning. Once I was away, I would be able to list the house for sale and move to a different city. I contacted some friends who said that I could stay with them. With these plans in place, I was waiting to leave on my business trip.

Tom came home in the early morning hours. It must have been one or two a.m. I peered out the bedroom window that overlooked the back entrance. I saw him stumbling as he came to the entrance. I saw that he was carrying something in his hands. As he opened the door, I called out to him, "Tom, are you OK?"

I got up from bed and met him at the door as he was coming in. He was carrying a towel wrapped around something. I strained my eyes to see what it was. The towel was masking what was inside.

He grabbed me and pulled me to the kitchen, where he pushed me onto a kitchen chair. "You sit there and don't move."

I was shaking and trying not to move, fearing that any movement on my part would cause him to start assaulting me.

His blurry eyes showed he was drunk or on drugs. He was walking back and forth across the kitchen. He started to unfold the towel. I saw a flash of steel, and then I saw the knife.

I didn't hesitate. I pushed the panic button on the necklace I was wearing.

Tom stood in front of me with the knife. I knew he was going to kill me. I could see he was trying to focus his eyes as he said, "You can't leave me."

He weaved to one side as he reached out to grab my arm. I saw the pain in his eyes as I swung towards him crying, "No, Tom, No." My arms flailed towards his face. My hand caught the knife.

He was stabbing me. I saw the blood and knew it was mine. Tom was the only one who heard my screams. I saw him reaching out to me as I heard the sirens and weakness overcame me. I felt myself falling.

The Judgement Game

1) What social issues are addressed in this vignette?

_____

_____

_____

2) What problems did Tom have?

_____

_____

_____

3) What problems did Fiona have?

_____

_____

_____

4) What role, if any, does gender play?

_____

_____

_____

5) Is there anything that might have prevented the problems you read about?

_____

_____

_____

6) Is the distinction between the offender and the victim clear?

Yes [   ]

No [   ]

COURT SUBMISSION

Case Number 52163-L

September 22, 2007

I make application for an eviction order, an occupational order, and a no-contact order against my estranged husband, Pierre Brun.

I have been separated from Pierre since August 6, 2006.

Pierre is French. I met Pierre when I went to Paris on vacation in May 2004. We were married in Blenham, Torcia in July of the same year. I had a job in Blenham, so we decided to purchase a house there. I had to pay the deposit on the house because Pierre was unemployed and had no savings. Pierre didn't speak English and wasn't able to find a job in Blenham, an English-speaking community. He had worked at part-time jobs as a waiter in Paris before we got married, and he convinced me it was a good idea to open a French restaurant in Blenham. It was planned that Pierre would operate the restaurant, and I would continue my work as a physiotherapist.

Pierre had been harassing me for over a month to make application to my bank for a loan to buy a building we could use for the restaurant business. I had made the application and the money was available for us. Pierre told me the previous day that he had a meeting with a real estate agent to complete the deal for the restaurant property. He said he would be taking $80,000 from our account for that purpose.

Bank records show that he withdrew $80,000 from our account on the morning of August 6. He took the money for his own use, not to purchase a property for our business. I learnt that he had been having an affair with another woman and had taken the woman on a trip to Rehna. They used the money on hotels, gambling, and entertainment. In fact, after he left the house on the sixth, he went to the bank, withdrew the money, and left with his girlfriend for Rehna.

By September, I knew he was not coming back to live with me. I started divorce proceedings and an application for distribution of matrimonial property. All proceedings were properly served on Pierre; however, he never filed defences or notices in response.

The Court made an interim order on November 1, 2006, providing that the matrimonial home be my place of residence until the divorce was finalised and matrimonial property proceedings were completed. (Interim Order of November 1, 2006)

I learnt from a common friend that Pierre's relationship with the other woman, Sarah, had not gone well. Sarah had also given Pierre money when he promised to open a restaurant business with her. The friend knew that this was the same promise Pierre had made to me and that both Sarah and I had been taken advantage of by Pierre. The friend gave me Sarah's telephone number, as he thought I might want to speak to her.

I didn't proceed with the divorce or matrimonial property action. I was in shock about what had happened to me and didn't want to face the reality that my marriage had failed. I wasn't able to avoid the situation for long, however, because on February 11, Pierre called me. He spoke as if he had never walked out on me, "Linda, my love, I am coming back so we can work out our property settlement. I want to deal with you alone, not with those bloodsucking serpent lawyers."

I agreed to see him, but after three meetings, it became clear that we couldn't agree on anything. If he did not get his way, he would bang his fist on the table and shout at me. The meetings did not resolve anything and caused me a great deal of fear and stress. I became frightened by the aggression he was showing. He was firm about his position. He wanted half of everything. I didn't believe he had the right to half of anything because I was the one who had accumulated everything and most of it before we were married. I asked Pierre not to call me again until he had a lawyer. That caused him to shout at me and call me a stupid bitch.

He paid no attention to my request not to call and phoned me again in June, saying, "Linda, I have to meet you right away. We have to settle things. I want this to be finished."

His voice sounded cold. I told him I wouldn't meet him unless he had a lawyer.

He shouted, "Greedy bitch" and hung up the phone.

Not long after the call, he started coming around the house uninvited. If I saw him coming, I hid and didn't answer the door. On a night in June, he came to the house and rang the doorbell. I didn't answer even when he banged on the door and shouted, "Let me in, Linda, I know you're inside. I want this over with"! I was frightened he would try to break the door down, but eventually he left.

I didn't call the police that night because I hadn't proceeded with the divorce and believed because of that, the Court would not help me. I did, however, call the "other woman". I told her who I was and said that Pierre had been coming around my house uninvited. I told her if she was still in touch with Pierre to tell him to leave me alone.

The woman, Sarah, didn't seem surprised to hear from me but was quick with her response, "I have a no-contact order against that bastard. He broke my arm; he threatened to kill me. I'm now deeply in debt because of the money he took from me to start a restaurant.

He also borrowed money from my parents that was never paid back. It was the most horrible relationship I have ever had. The man has no scruples. I want nothing to do with the son of a bitch."

She continued talking. "In Rehna I was his princess. Nothing was too expensive for lovely Sarah. After I gave him the money to start the restaurant business things changed. Our relationship became intolerable. He was aggressive and critical, telling me that I had no business sense and that is why we had no customers. The verbal abuse became more frequent and in June, during a fight about money, he hit me in the face and broke my arm. He threatened to kill me. A neighbour heard my screams and called the police. Pierre was arrested and charged with uttering a death threat and assault causing bodily harm. I know he has been released and is somewhere here in Blenham."

With a sigh, she said, "I don't know where he is. All I can do now is go to Court and tell the judge what he did to me." Sarah went on to say I could use the information about what happened to her if I needed to.

I was shocked to hear what Pierre had done to her and given his actions the previous evening, I immediately contacted the police. I was told to attend the Blenham Police Station to file a complaint.

I attended the station and explained my concerns for my personal safety because of Pierre's harassment. As a result of my attendance, Report 63089, was filed.

I returned home to find that Pierre had left messages on my voice mail demanding I meet with him immediately. I received another call on June 14 that I didn't answer because I suspected it was Pierre. I was right. He left another voice message: "Linda, we must meet at the house. Darling, I need your help."

I returned to the police station that day and filed a second report, "Report 63089-2. I was frightened by Pierre's message. I arranged to have the police escort me back to the house. Sure enough, Pierre was waiting outside the door. The police officer didn't hesitate. Once he confirmed that it was Pierre, the officer arrested him immediately. I subsequently found out he was held overnight and the next day, when released, given a harassment warning and cautioned not to go back to the house.

Despite the warning, Pierre continued to hang around the area where I lived. I saw him walking along the street, but he did not come to the house. It did not take long, however, before Pierre ignored the warning completely.

On July 11, I saw him approaching the house. I called the emergency contact number given to me by the police. Pierre arrived at the house and rang the buzzer. I didn't answer the door and waited for the arrival of the police. Fortunately, they came quickly and Pierre was arrested. That arrest led to the Court granting a no-contact order[1] on July 12. Even with the no-contact order, I was concerned that Pierre continued to remain at liberty and was able to walk the streets freely. I felt a prisoner in my own neighbourhood. I had no idea when Pierre might decide to breach the order, and I feared for my safety.

My stress level was so high that at the end of July, I decided to leave Blenham for a month. During the month, I left the house vacant. I asked neighbours to watch the house for me and let me know if Pierre tried to return.

In late August, I received a Facebook message telling me Pierre had moved back into the house. Apparently, he had hired a locksmith and moved back on August 26.

I returned to Blenham on the September long weekend. I have been staying with friends. I couldn't go back to my house because I knew Pierre was living there. I cannot believe what has happened to me; I cannot return to my own home because of my fear.

I have come to Court for assistance. I ask that you grant the orders I have requested: an eviction order, an occupational order, and a no-contact order.

---

1 See Annex B for definition of no- contact order.

I hope I have provided enough information to explain my situation. I also want you to know I have continued to make all payments for the mortgage, utilities, and insurance. Pierre has not contributed anything. He is back in the house and has access to all of my personal documents, my computer, my furniture, everything. The most important thing, however, is that I am frightened for my safety.

Linda Brun (Garnett)

The Judgement Game
1) What orders do you feel the Court should have made:

   Eviction order: Yes [ ] No [ ]

   Occupation order: Yes [ ] No [ ]

   No-contact order: Yes [ ] No [ ]

2) Do you believe one of the following responses would be appropriate?

   Probation with counselling
   for the offender: Yes [ ] No [ ]

   Incarceration of the offender: Yes [ ] No [ ]

   Do you suggest another type of solution to deal with the problem?

   _____

   _____

   _____

3) Is the distinction between the offender and the victim clear?
   Yes [ ]

   No [ ]

REBECA AND DAVE

The first time I saw him, it was the beauty of his body that attracted my attention. I was mesmerised by him. He entered the gym wearing only gym shorts and joggers. Without his shirt, his sculpted arms and biceps were reminiscent of the marble statues of Rodin. Some might think the shape too perfect, every limb tanned and every muscle defined. There was, however, something rough and untamed about him that I found appealing. The raw sexuality of the man caused me to stop my gaze from going lower. I knew I was invading his world.

I give lessons in Internet technology for the company, Hanton Computer Systems. I was at Sportco, one of Hanton's customers, where I was giving an IT seminar to fitness instructors about the new computer system Sportco had installed. My initial thought was, what am I doing? What is wrong with me? Why can't I be satisfied with my husband, Robert?

Robert is a judge and well known in the city. Yesterday had been the standard Friday routine. A quickie before dinner. A "Friday-afternoon quickie" was what Robert wanted. It was always the same. When he came back from Court on Friday afternoons, sex was on his mind. Perhaps he found it arousing to touch me after listening to people fighting about money all afternoon.

We always had sex before we went for dinner. For me it was sex, not making love. In fact, I found it rather annoying and distasteful, as I felt I hadn't enough time to take a relaxing shower before getting dressed for dinner. It was always a rush, a quickie, a fast shower, and then just enough time to grab something to wear before we had to leave.

When I got to the Sportco lecture room where I was giving the class, the Rodin man was sitting in the front row. He was now dressed in a T-shirt and jeans and looked even more appealing than before. There was ruggedness in his manner that I found intriguing. He was waiting to hear my IT lecture. Our eyes met and there was an unspoken contact. I wanted to learn more about him, and I could tell from his glance he wanted to learn more about me.

After the class, he stopped to tell me that he had enjoyed the lecture and asked me a question about the capability of the new computers. I learnt his name was Dave. His question required me to obtain information from the distributor of the computers. That gave me an opportunity to exchange telephone numbers, which I was happy to do. That meant I would have the ability to contact him. I could tell from his eyes that he was interested in me.

I went home to get ready for Friday-night dinner with Robert and a group of his lawyer friends. It had been a long day with my work at Hanton, and I was still mulling over the incident with Dave. I just wanted to get the sex bit with Robert over with, have a shower, and dress for dinner. I didn't know what was wrong with me. I knew I should have been happy with Robert; he was a loving husband. He was attentive to me. He was blond and slim with a boy next-door type of charm. I couldn't define what was missing. It was, perhaps, the element of mystery and intrigue that Dave had.

Although it was the same routine, something caused Robert to realise I was not responding to his caresses. After we had sex, he leaned over and said, "Rebeca, are you happy? Your beautiful eyes look distant tonight. I hope I pleased you, dear. You didn't seem to relax."

I was a good actor and managed to say my lines with passion and skill. He would not understand if I told him the truth, which was that I was tired and sex was the last thing on my mind that evening. My script was good: "Bob, I love my work, but I love you more." That seemed to satisfy him.

Dave called me the following week. He invited me for a glass of wine at a restaurant near the Sportco office. My heart soared. I cancelled my manicure appointment so I could meet him.

One glass of wine led to another, and after four hours of being together, he asked if I wanted to come back to his apartment so he could show me the medals he'd won. I really didn't care what reason he gave me, I was happy to be invited to his apartment. I knew I didn't have to go home that night because Robert was at a judicial conference out of the city. I happily accepted Dave's invitation.

The evening turned into one of ecstasy. Dave awakened sexual desires I had never experienced before. I felt as though our bodies became one. He filled me with his sperm and I experienced profound orgasms. Dave's passion brought me such pleasure. I could finally say I was making love.

Following that magical evening, we met at his apartment each Saturday. Robert always went to his office on Saturdays, and I told him I was taking a class at the gym.

Dave wanted more than weekend flings, but that was all I could give him. I didn't want my comfortable life with Robert to be disrupted. Dave kept asking me to divorce Robert and suggested that we start a relationship together with the money he had saved from his job as a fitness instructor and the money I would obtain from a matrimonial settlement with Robert. He wanted us to build a new life together, but I kept stalling, telling him I needed more time.

I arrived at his apartment one Saturday ready for my weekly lovemaking fix. My sexual experience with Dave had become an addiction. Once I had tasted the pleasure, I wanted more.

Dave was sullen. It seemed something had changed. After I sat down, he asked me if I had made love with Robert that week, something he had never asked me before. I told him I was there for him and did not want to talk about my life with Robert. That did not satisfy him and he kept pushing me with his questions. "Is Robert a good lover? Does he give you what I do"?

I did not respond. He continued: "I asked you if Robert is a good lover."

I didn't respond. I thought it best we end the conversation and the afternoon. I told him I needed to leave to do some shopping. I didn't know what else to say.

I tried to stand up so I could leave. He stood above me and held my shoulders so I couldn't get up. He had never acted like this before.

I started to cry. He grabbed my arm and twisted it behind my back. When I screamed, he started hitting me. He was a strong man and although I tried to struggle, I didn't have a chance. The next thing I remember was seeing a police officer standing in front of me.

My forehead was bleeding. My left arm was throbbing in excruciating pain. I couldn't remember exactly what happened. I must have passed out and been left alone at the apartment.

I found out at the hospital that my arm was broken. It was in a cast for three months. My face has healed, but I will have a scar above my left eye.

Robert found out about the assault because the police called him when I was taken to the hospital. The police found my diary in my purse. The diary had an emergency number to contact; it was Robert's office number.

When Robert was told where I was, he came to the hospital. The police must have explained where they found me because Robert didn't ask me any questions. His manner was cold. His only words to me were, "Rebeca, I loved you. How could you have cheated"?

He took me home from the hospital, but did not want to talk to me. That was the end of our relationship. There was little conversation and we did not go out for dinner or have sexual relations again.

Dave was charged with assault causing bodily harm. I received a subpoena and had to attend Court to testify against him. It was hard for me to talk about what had happened. In fact, I can't believe it happened. I told the Court what I was able to remember of my last day at Dave's apartment. I was not cross-examined by

DANCING WITH A LEOPARD— CASES OF DOMESTIC ABUSE

Dave's lawyer. It was clear he had given the lawyer instructions not to cross-examine me. Robert did not attend Court, likely, because he didn't want to see the man who had been my lover and who had assaulted me.

Dave's lawyer told the Court that Dave had no previous criminal record. Despite that information, new legislation attempting to stop violence against women made it mandatory that Dave be sent to jail. The judge gave him a sentence of three months of incarceration without any right to have the time reduced.

I know I will never see Dave again. I don't want to see him. He destroyed my life.

Robert filed for divorce and division of matrimonial property. I will be given a lucrative property settlement, but I will be alone. I will have no husband and I am now the scarlet woman of the legal community.

I know what I did was wrong but my punishment is not fair. The loss of my husband and my friends is too much. I do not deserve this.

The Judgement Game
1) What social issues are addressed in this vignette?

_____

_____

_____

2) What problems did Rebeca have?

_____

_____

_____

3) What problems did Dave have?

_____

_____

_____

4) What role, if any, does gender play?

_____

_____

_____

5) Is there anything that might have prevented the problems you read about?

_____

_____

_____

6) Is the distinction between offender and victim clear?

Yes ☐

No ☐

CLAUDE AND DEBBIE

Claude would do anything to have contact with his ex-girlfriend, Debbie. Before the no-contact order, he and Debbie had been together for six years. He loved Debbie and wanted her back.

He managed to save enough money to return to Torcia from Gabot, a country in the Middle East. He had been conducting pipeline surveys for the gas-line service company he was working for.

Claude had flown back to Torcia from Gabot. It was a long journey and he was exhausted from the travel. He had taken a flight from Gabot to Amsterdam and then to Jervis. He still had the keys to his house in Jervis, the house where he and Debbie had lived prior to the incident that caused him to leave for Gabot.

He knew Debbie had been granted a no-contact order against him stating he was to have no contact with her and that he could not return to their house.

When he arrived in Jervis, he decided that Debbie had probably forgiven him for the incident and he would go to the house to see her. He would arrange for her to come to Court with him to have the no-contact order removed.

When he arrived at the airport, he took a taxi to his house. Unfortunately, when he tried to open the front door, he found the lock had been changed. He rang the doorbell but nobody answered. He walked around the house to look through the windows but there did not appear to be anyone home.

He went next door and talked to his neighbour, Elaine, who told him Debbie had been at her house earlier that morning. She said Debbie told her she was going to visit her mother that afternoon.

Claude was so eager to talk to Debbie he asked Elaine if he could use her telephone to call Debbie's mother. Elaine let him use the phone and Claude made the call. He spoke to Debbie briefly, "Debbie, I'm home. I've come back to be with you. "

Debbie's response was abrupt. "You have no right to call me. I have an order against you. You have no right to be at the house." She hung up the phone.

Claude was upset that she didn't want to talk to him. He had come so far and he was not going to stop without going to the house to see her. He thanked Elaine and went back to his house.

Claude thought it possible that the key he had would still open the garage door. He went to the garage and tried to open the door. That lock had also been changed. He was furious. "Shit, this is my house! This is my garage"!

Claude had hidden some drugs in the garage and wanted to pick them up. He kicked the door of the garage open and went inside to see if the drugs were still there. They were. He found the bag of marijuana exactly where he had left it. He smoked some marijuana to calm himself and put the rest in his backpack.

Claude was in a dream world. Memories came flooding back to him about the last time he had been at the house. His mind was in a haze.

He felt Debbie's lips on his. She was kissing him. He remembered something bad had happened. He saw her standing in front of him. He was reaching out to touch her. Debbie's face darkened. He knew she was going to hit him. He saw her falling. He was running.

Claude focused his mind. He had come back for Debbie. He loves Debbie. They had been together for six years and had a terrific relationship. The problem was the booze and the drugs, he needed them. He needed Debbie.

He had been drinking the day the incident happened. He'd been with friends at a football game and hadn't gone back to his house until late in the evening. He hadn't called Debbie all day to let her know where he was.

Debbie had been waiting for him to come home. She started crying when he arrived at the house and she saw he was drunk. She accused him of not having called her and called him a thoughtless, selfish drunk. He became angry and told her to leave him alone. He recalls her coming toward him with clenched fists. He remembers reaching out to push her away. He remembers her falling. He panicked, ran out of the house and drove away.

Debbie must have called the police because he remembers the flashing lights of the police car behind him. He knew he was drunk and tried to avoid the police by racing at high speeds and using back alleys in an attempt to escape. His car hit another vehicle as he was going through an intersection and he had no choice but to stop to face the music.

He was arrested and taken to the police station. He was charged with assault of a partner, criminal endangerment and impaired driving. He was placed in custody overnight and released the next day on his promise to attend Court. He was given an appearance notice indicating the day he was to return to Court. He never attended Court on the day that had been scheduled. He had been working in Gabot.

Claude focuses on his present situation. He looks out the window of the garage and sees a police car driving toward the house. He watches as an officer gets out of the car. He realises there is no way for him to escape. He is alone in the garage.

He left the garage to speak to the officer who said, "You are not to be at this residence. You know that, don't you"?

Claude replied to the officer, "I know I'm not supposed to be here, but it is my house and I only wanted to pick up a few personal items. No one is at home." The officer told him that did not matter and arrested and charged him.

Claude knew he was in more trouble now than he had been when he'd left Jervis a few months ago. He decided to enter guilty pleas to the charges against him. He thought there would be less publicity if he entered guilty pleas. A trial would attract the media and he did not want that kind of publicity or stress. He knew that he was guilty of the offences and wanted to get it over with rather than going to trial.

Claude entered guilty pleas to the charges that had been filed before he left for Gabot:
- Assault of Partner;

Note: Torcian law imposes a minimum sentence of three months imprisonment for assault of a partner.
- Criminal Endangerment;
- Impaired Driving.

He also entered guilty pleas to the new charges of:
- Failure to attend Court;
- Breach of the No-contact order; and
- Possession of marijuana (found in Claude's backpack).

After hearing the submissions of the lawyer for the State of Torcia, the judge asked Claude if he had anything he wished to say.

Claude made the following comments:

"Everything I did was for the cause of love. I love Debbie and I know Debbie still loves me. She can't turn her back on me. I will get her back."

The Judgement Game

1) What social issues are addressed in this vignette?

_____

_____

_____

2) What problems did Claude have?

_____

_____

_____

3) What problems did Debbie have?

_____

_____

_____

4) What role, if any, does gender play?

_____

_____

_____

5) Is there anything that might have prevented the problems you read about?

_____

_____

_____

6) Is the distinction between offender and victim clear?

Yes ☐

No ☐

Self-Assessment

You have the opportunity to provide a self-assessment after reading the vignettes in "Dancing with a Leopard: Domestic Violence."

Indicate how many points* you give yourself for:

1) Recognition of issues raised in the chapter. ___

2) Suggestions and comments you made. ___

3) Your role as a decision maker. ___

TOTAL: ___

*You can give yourself 0 (lowest) to 5 (highest) points.
This is a game. Remember there are no right or wrong answers.

CHAPTER 2:
FAMILY AFFAIRS

• • •

The vignettes in this chapter involve both civil and criminal cases. Civil cases involve two different parties. One party, the Plaintiff, commences an action against another party, the Defendant. Criminal cases are actions by the State of Torcia against an individual for committing a criminal offence as defined by Torcia's criminal law.

SIBLING PLAY

I'm Hank. I use my Harley to pick up chicks. I like to score with them free, but if I need some lovin', I'm willing to pay to get my rocks off. If she is worth paying, I'll drop a hundred bucks for the full meal deal. If she isn't worth it, I don't pay. I was once charged with theft when the bitch went to the police because I didn't pay, but I'd rather spend a few days in jail than pay for a worthless trick.

I'll pay up to fifty bucks for a good blowjob. I like young flesh and often search for young meat standing by the river waiting for tricks. They'll give me a blowjob for twenty bucks, cheaper than downtown, where I have to cough up fifty.

When we finish work, I like to talk trash, a load of bullshit, with my buddies over a cold beer. We are roofers and it's a tough and dirty job. When the job is finished, we like to let loose and relax. I am one of the guys with the most stories to tell. Most of the stories are true but others are things I've read in the sex magazines I buy every week. There is, however, one story I never tell. It is the story about my sister, Jeannie.

It happened when we were children. I am older than Jeannie is. I had just turned seventeen and Jeannie was seven. I was starting to feel like a man. I would wake up at night with a hard-on and would satisfy myself with my hand.

One day when Jeannie and I were playing hide-and-seek, I suggested she follow me downstairs to my room in the basement. I slept in the basement because it was cooler and I liked the privacy. Jeannie was happy to spend time with me. When we were together, she always called me "Big Brother Hank."

I turned the lights off to make sure that no one knew we were in the basement. I really didn't mean to ask her to touch my private parts, but I couldn't resist. I asked her to play with my cock. It got harder and harder until I let the juice flow. Jeannie told me she did not like this game because it was messy. I said that she was right, the game was too messy, and we wouldn't play the game again.

The following week Jeannie asked me if I had any games to play with her. I did not want to go to the basement again, but she wanted to play games and the basement was the best place to play. At first, we played "blind man's bluff." I then started to play the same game we had played the previous week. She said, "Hank, don't you have any other games? You promised me a new game."

I told her, "Jeannie, you can watch me play the game alone or you can play as well. It won't be messy if you just choose to watch. It's up to you."

Jeannie decided to watch me play the game alone. Everything was all right until something came over me. I got angry that she was watching me and didn't want to play.

"Jeannie, if you want to be with me, you have to play."

My mind isn't clear about exactly what happened, but I know I did something I have regretted for the rest of my life. The scream was horrible when it happened. I do not know if it was her scream or if it was mine.

I never told this story to the boys. I never asked Jeannie to come to play in the basement again. She asked me later why I didn´t love her anymore and why I didn't want to be her friend. She had forgiven me but I had not forgiven myself and never will. I fucked my little sister that day in the basement.

Jeannie grew up to be a beautiful woman. Heads turn when she walks by. She's a commercial sales representative for an international gas service company. She's one of the smart ones who managed to get out of our neighbourhood. She is now living in the Everglades, the posh part of the city. It is the same city where we grew up, but it might as well be two separate cities—the rough area where we grew up and the big houses in the Everglades.

I left that city behind me. I couldn't face meeting her on the streets. I went to a different city to find a job.

Because I didn't do well in school, the only jobs I could get were labouring jobs. I was good at building things, so I took a job working for a contractor. I thought about starting my own business but that didn't work out. I stole some lumber from the boss to build a shed for my Harley and my boss found out. I did time in jail, and when I got out of jail, the only work I could find was some casual work as a roofer. It's alright I suppose. I can take on jobs when times are good and go on the dole when there isn't any work around. It works well for me because I don't have to stay in one place for very long. Working as a labourer lets me move from one city to another.

Jeannie and I are brother and sister, but we don't speak about the past. When we meet on family occasions, we talk about current events, the weather, the news and our jobs.

I worry that she will go to the police and lay charges against me for sexual assault. I've heard that people can lay charges for sexual offences that happened to them in the past. I am haunted by my fear of what happened that afternoon in the basement.

I can't forget the scream. Jeannie can still go to the police.

The Judgement Game

1) What social problems addressed in the vignette, "Sibling Play"?

_____

_____

_____

2) If Hank were found guilty of sexual assault, what punishment would you impose?

*In Torcia, sexual assault has a maximum penalty of ten years imprisonment. There is no minimum penalty.

_____

_____

_____

CAROLE, RON AND FAMILY

Information Provided by Carole

We were married for seven years. We have two children, Sam and Alan. Sam is nine years old. He was born before I married Ron. He is Ron's child but came as a surprise. Likely, this surprise is what sparked Ron's proposal to get married.

Alan is seven years old. He is definitely Ron's child; he is a carbon copy of his dad.

I was happy enough for the first five years I was with Ron. He would buy me many presents: perfume, flowers, and beautiful jewellery. He would take me out for dinner at least once a week.

Ron is an accountant with an international firm. He spends most of his time at work and when he does come home, all he wants to do is relax and watch television with Sam and Alan. He likes to take the boys to baseball and hockey games on the weekends. I was never invited to go with them. Ron called those events "boys' day out."

What had initially attracted me to Ron was that he made me feel important and loved. His friends are important people in the city, so being with Ron in public also made me feel important. I know my education is not as good as Ron's, but that didn't seem to matter in the beginning. I have a degree in education and worked for two years as a primary schoolteacher before Sam was born. After we were married, we decided that I would stop working and become a stay-at-home mom.

I thought I would be able to convince Ron to take an interest in the things I enjoyed. Unfortunately, that didn't happen. Our lives became routine. He went to work and I pursued my own interests and looked after the children.

After seven years of marriage, I realised the flame of love had gone out. I finally acknowledged we had nothing in common. I enjoy sewing, cooking, and playing tennis. Ron didn't do any cooking and never wanted to learn how to play tennis. His only interest was working, watching baseball and hockey games on television or going to the games.

Our sex life had become the pits. Making love became routine, generally once a week. Most of the time, Ron wanted to make love on Sunday mornings before the hockey and baseball games started on television.

It was my decision to end the marriage. I retained a female lawyer, Nicole Brown, to represent me. I believed I would have a better chance to win my claim for custody if my lawyer was a woman. I thought she would understand my situation better than a man would.

Ms Brown told me that if Ron and I lived separately, it would take me a year to get the divorce. She said that obtaining the divorce was the easy part, and it was the matter of custody that would be more difficult.

I told her it was important for me that I obtain sole custody. In response, she told me that Courts favour awards of joint custody and I would need to show the Court special circumstances why I should be granted sole custody. She said the Court looks at the question: "what is in the best interests of the children" in making its decision. I told her that it seemed to me that it would be in the best interests of the children to be with their mother. Ms Brown indicated that is not always the case.

The reason I wanted sole custody is that Ron and I have very different views about how to bring up children. I believe in exercising discipline and Ron doesn't. He believes one should never use corporal punishment, such as spanking a child for things the child has done wrong. I believe that sometimes there is no alternative but to threaten or to use such punishment.

As well, our beliefs about religion and education are completely different. I want the boys to go to a private bilingual school; Ron wants them to attend a public school in the city. I am an atheist and do not want my children to be brainwashed by churches. Ron comes from a religious background and believes the boys should go to church.

Ron applied for joint custody. He believes we should be able to make decisions together. I know that is not possible because our beliefs are too different.

I decided I had to put myself in a better position than Ron in order to win the custody battle. I know Ron has more money than I do and I felt I needed to level the playing field in some other way.

I read an article in a developmental psychology magazine discussing the idea of imprinting. The article convinced me that I needed to show the Court that I had built a positive bond with the boys so that custody would be awarded to me. My idea was to do things to convince the boys that I was the best parent so they would tell the Court they wanted to stay with me.

I started by buying gifts for the boys that would move them away from interests such as baseball and hockey that they had been pursuing with Ron. I decided to give them tennis and French lessons. I also began saying negative things about Ron to the boys. I told them that Ron wasn't nice to me anymore. I said he shouted at me and would hit me when he felt I had done something wrong. The boys seemed surprised by this, but I saw they were listening and watching my interaction with Ron. I made sure I acted unhappy when I was with Ron and tried to act as if I was frightened of him when the boys saw us together. I inflicted bruises on my arms and wore short sleeves to make sure the boys would notice the bruises. I saw the children were upset by what I was telling them and started to distance themselves from Ron.

Ron didn't understand what was happening and suggested we see a psychologist. He told me he wanted to repair our relationship because he still loved me. He said he felt he'd done something wrong because he was working too much and not paying enough attention to me.

I didn't want to repair our relationship but decided to play along with him during the one year necessary to obtain the divorce. I was also able to convince Ron that I needed to spend time alone and he should rent an apartment. My reason for doing that was to allow me to stay in the matrimonial home with the boys and to separate them from Ron. In trade for him moving to an apartment, I agreed we could see psychologists, separate psychologists for each of us.

When I saw my psychologist, I told her that Ron had abused me emotionally by saying that I was stupid and a bad role model for the boys because of our differences about religion and education. I also told her Ron would hit me when we were arguing. I knew I was exaggerating but sometimes Ron did raise his fists and shout at me.

When Ron rented his apartment, he asked to see the boys once a week and on alternate weekends. I consented but was concerned that Ron would try to turn the boys against me. Because of my fear, I told the boys that their father only wanted to spend time with them to hurt me. I think Alan believed what I was saying because he refused to go to Ron's apartment. Sam went to Ron's apartment once a week and on alternate weekends, but never talked to me about what he and his father had done together on his visits.

On one occasion, Sam started a fire in Ron's study that caused a significant amount of damage. A neighbour called the police and fire brigade. The police investigation showed Sam had planned this event in advance and purposely taken kerosene and matches to set the fire.

The police wanted to lay charges of arson against Sam for the incident because of his intent to cause damage and the danger his actions caused, not only to Ron, but also to other residents of the building. Ron convinced the police not to lay charges by telling them that Sam's actions were not normal but a result of the custody battle in which Ron and I were involved. Fortunately, the police did not lay a charge of arson against Sam.

Ron was extremely upset about what Sam had done and told me that the divorce was not only destroying his relationship with his sons but also causing Sam to become aggressive. He blamed me for starting the divorce proceedings and fighting with him about custody. Despite the fire incident, Ron continued his weekly meetings with Sam.

The divorce was granted. The custody matter is still before the Court.

I provided an affidavit to the Court indicating that Ron emotionally and physically abused me. I knew I was exaggerating the situation. I did that in order to win the custody battle. Ron's lawyer cross-examined me on my affidavit but I stuck to my story. My motto is that all is fair in love, war, and custody battles.

I don't understand why this has become so twisted and complicated. Sam and Alan are my children. I believe that should be enough. Instead, I am caught in a maze controlled by lawyers, psychologists and the Court. All I am trying to do is to level the playing field so that I can have custody of my sons.

Information Provided by Ron
Ron filed an affidavit stating he did not emotionally or physically abuse Carole. He seeks joint custody of the children and costs against Carole in the custody action.

Court Decision
The Court asks for more information on the matter of custody. It wants information on the question "what is in the best interests of the children." It has instructed an independent Court appointed social worker to review the material presented in this report and to make a determination about that question.

Your Role
You are the Court appointed social worker and will provide an evaluation based on the information provided in this report. You will decide what issues need to be considered in determining "what is in the best interests of the children." You will also make a recommendation to the Court regarding which parent or parents should be granted custody of Sam and Alan. The Court will act based on your recommendation. You will also determine whether the Court should penalize either parent for his or her actions in this legal proceeding. Penalties can be awarded by making an order that one of the parties pay Court costs and/ or solicitor-client costs of the opposing party's lawyer. You will be provided information about the amount of costs that can be awarded. You will also decide if costs are a sufficient response to the actions of the parties in this case.

The Judgement Game

1) In the vignette "Carole, Ron, and family," what do you, the Court appointed social worker, believe is " in the best interests of the children"?

_____
_____
_____

2) As the Court appointed social worker, what recommendation do you make to the Court regarding custody of the boys?

_____
_____
_____

3) In the vignette "Carole, Ron, and family", do you recommend the Court impose penalties (Court costs and/ or solicitor-client costs)[2] against any of the parties?

_____
_____
_____

(a) If so, which party or parties?

_____
_____
_____

(b) Are costs a sufficient penalty?

Yes ☐
No ☐

---

2 In the case of Carole, Ron and Family, *The Judgement Game* sets Court Costs at $200, being costs for the Court's services. *The Judgement Game* sets Solicitor/ Client costs at $1,500, being costs allowed by the Court for the legal services of each party. This does not represent the legal fees paid by Carole and Ron to their lawyers.

(c) If not, what is your suggestion?

_____

_____

_____

FAMILY DUTIES OF KADAR MOHAT

It was my duty to bring my father to Torcia. I am his only son and the only child in the family. I emigrated to Torcia ten years ago and work for a publishing firm in Torcia. I have been successful in my job, and compared to the standard of living of my parents and relatives in Filo, my home country, I am considered a wealthy person. I had enough money to bring my seventy-two year old father to my new country.

Father left mother for a period of time to live with another woman in Filo. It was the custom in Filo that he could have affairs with other women. I learnt that father had lived with three different women during the time he had been married to mother. Mother was often left on her own and had to be cared for by me, her brothers and sisters and neighbours in her community. I did not agree with these customs, but it was my obligation to respect my parents and their customs.

I learnt father had abused my mother when he lived with her. Her neighbour told me that mother had often gone to her house with bruises and on one occasion with cuts on her face. Mother did not report the crimes because she had been taught that a wife had to accept her husband the way he was. I understand that many women in Filo are abused by their husbands but do not speak about the abuse.

When Father became ill, he moved back with mother. She took him back and provided care for him even though he had been unfaithful to her for many years.

Mother passed away two years ago. Morally, I can not accept the way my father had treated my mother but the only thing I have been able to do to appease my conscious has been to provide financial support to a human rights organization taking steps to draft legislation for Filo and other countries to stop violence against women.

When mother died, one of her neighbours contacted me and said that I should bring father to Torcia because there was no one to look after him in Filo. She said it was my duty to bring him to Torcia.

It was not easy for me to bring father to Torcia, either morally or practically. The reality of father's situation was that he had significant medical problems. His doctors in Filo told me he had significant heart and respiratory problems and had recently undergone an operation for colon cancer. I was provided information from the doctors in Filo that he had a lengthy medical history and it was their opinion that he was likely to have ongoing medical problems. Despite this information, I made an application to bring my father to Torcia.

Torcia´s health authorities told me they would oppose my application because they did not want to pay potential costs for bringing unhealthy people to Torcia. As a result, Torcia´s immigration appeals tribunal had to make the decision. I accepted that I needed to look after my father in his final years so pursued my application.

I succeeded at the immigration tribunal. That decision allowed me to bring father to Torcia.

Father lived with me for three years. I hired caregivers for each of the three years with half of the cost being paid by me and the other half being paid for by the State of Torcia because of legislation to help the elderly. After the three years of living at my home, father was admitted to hospital for respiratory problems. He died after spending six months in intensive care at one of Torcia's hospitals.

I fulfilled my family duty. I must, however, live with my father's crimes for the rest of my life.

The Judgement Game

1) Did the immigration authorities do the right thing in allowing Kadar Mohat to bring his father to Torcia?

Yes ☐

No ☐

2) What would you have done?

_____
_____
_____

3) What were his father's crimes?

_____
_____
_____

LOOKING FOR OSCAR

What did I do to deserve this man?

I met Oscar at a rodeo. I was one of the girls riding in the opening ceremony. I was young, having just turned seventeen. I was chosen as Rodeo Princess based on my personality and on having good equestrian skills. I had won first place in the western cutting competition for Torcia the previous year and this year was a finalist in the sport of mounted shooting.

I was dressed in Western clothing, wearing tight jeans and a short flashy sequined top that accentuated my bust. My long blond hair was caught up with a diamond coloured barrette. I know I looked like a princess that day.

Following the opening ceremony, my brother Ben took me over to introduce me to Oscar. Oscar had just purchased cattle from Ben who was discussing selling more cattle to him.

After the introduction, Ben told me Oscar had asked him whether "the little princess" was also for sale. When I heard what they had been talking about I told my brother they were both sexist and I did not find their joke funny. My brother laughed and said, "Don't worry, I told him you are a proud princess and not for sale." I knew that they had been joking but I admit it made me pay more attention to Oscar.

I learnt Oscar was a wealthy man who owned a large cattle ranch. He raised horses, one of my major interests. He was tall and blond and looked like the cowboy movie star, Robbie Hanson, from my favourite television programme, *Callas*. I found him attractive but learnt he was at least ten years older than I was.

At the rodeo dance that evening, Oscar invited me to dance. He was nice but not very romantic. He tried to touch my breasts when we were dancing and kept patting me on my bottom when I would turn around. My long golden braids had fallen out of the barrette and Oscar reached over to take the braids and twirl me around with them. I lost my balance and he had to hold me up to keep me from falling. He seemed to enjoy having to rescue me.

Although other men wanted me to dance with them, Oscar kept coming over to bring me beer and ask me for another dance. It was clear he was interested in me.

At the end of the night, Oscar invited me to come to see his ranch. The idea appealed to me. I had heard he lived in a large house like the ones I'd seen on Callus. I was curious. The beer had gone to my head and I accepted his invitation.

I was impressed with the ranch house. It was older and looked even larger than the one on the television programme Callus. Oscar showed me the medals he had won at rodeos and horse shows. I was in awe. I had found a cowboy and my own "prince charming".

Oscar lived three hours from the town where the rodeo was held and the dance had ended at midnight. He seemed to take it for granted that accepting his invitation meant I would stay at the ranch house. He didn't ask but merely said, "I'll drive you back to town in the morning." I must say I had been swept off my feet by his attention and his invitation. I didn't know what else to do but accept. He didn't talk about where I would be sleeping; he just took me with him to his bedroom.

Oscar was true to his word and drove me back to town the next day. When he dropped me off, his parting words were, "be seeing you, little princess." Little princess is all he ever called me, although he knew my name.

I was only with him that one night, but as fate would have it, I became pregnant. When I told my family I was pregnant, Ben called me to say that he would get in touch with Oscar. Ben said he would tell Oscar to do the right thing by me, meaning to marry me. I told Ben that in the modern world the man does not have to marry the woman just because she gets pregnant. Ben disagreed and told me that it was a question of morality and financial responsibility. Ben's conclusion was that if you sleep with a woman and she gets pregnant, you must accept the consequences. For Ben, the consequences were marriage and financial responsibility for the wife and child.

Ben obviously talked to Oscar because Oscar called me the next day. His first comment to me was, "Ben called me yesterday. Why do you think it's my baby"? That upset me because Oscar was the first and only man I'd slept with. When I told him that, he seemed surprised. After many tears and pleas on my part, Oscar accepted that it was his baby.

Oscar came to town to see me and told me that he would look after the baby and me but would not marry me. He told me he had been married before and it hadn't been a good experience. Oscar was an only child. He was spoiled by his parents and had little incentive to work. He hired workers to look after the cattle and horses on the ranch. I learnt from Oscar that his ex-wife was chasing him for spousal maintenance and maintenance for her children. He told me they had two children. He did not want to talk about his life with his ex-wife or about his children.

I moved to the ranch during my pregnancy. Oscar was attentive and loving during my pregnancy. After the baby was born, I stayed at the ranch to look after the baby.

After five years together, Oscar and I had three children, two daughters and a son, Isobel, Evie and Jacob. Oscar would often come barrelling in to the ranch with boxes of chocolates or perfume for me and toys for the children. I felt things were going well for us. I accepted that Oscar didn't want to be married but believed he loved me. I trusted he would always stay with our children and me.

Later that year, I found out something had changed. Oscar started spending more time away from the ranch. He said he needed to be away so that he could follow the rodeo circuit and take part in the rodeo event of steer wrestling.

I learnt that Oscar had been spending time in Jervis, the city where he had gone to agricultural college. I found this out when I was contacted by the Jervis police who were looking for Oscar. He had lent his car, a new Corvette, to his friend, Kevin. Unfortunately, Kevin was in a car accident while driving the car. The police had arrested Kevin after the accident. He was charged with several offences, one of which was possession of cocaine. The police called me to find out if Oscar was home because they wanted to speak to him. I told them that Oscar was not home but didn't mention that he hadn't been home for the past three months. I thought it best not to say more to the police.

Oscar missed Isobel's birthday and never even called to wish her happy birthday. I tried to contact him on his cellular phone, but the message on the phone indicated that the storage was full. I had no idea where Oscar was or how to get in touch with him.

It wasn't long before I found out from people in the neighbourhood that Oscar had been living with Kevin for the past three months. I learnt that Oscar had been obtaining money from a trust distributed by lawyers in Reda for a class action commenced by a group of ranchers, including Oscar. The Reda lawyers were distributing the settlement funds monthly. I also found out Oscar had recently left Torcia. It was unknown where he had gone.

The Reda lawyers are looking for Oscar because they need to distribute funds that have been accumulating in trust for him for the past three months.

The police are looking for Oscar because they found cocaine in a jacket Oscar left at one of the rodeo events he recently attended.

Family Enforcement is looking for Oscar because he is several months in arrears for payments to his ex-wife and her children.

I am looking for Oscar to tell him I am not a Princess and he is not Prince Charming. I am a middle-aged woman with three children and Oscar is a common toad without either morality or a sense of financial responsibility.

The Judgement Game
1) What solution would you recommend to deal with Oscar?

_____

_____

_____

2) Should Oscar return to Torcia, what sentence would you impose on Oscar for the offence of possession of cocaine?
Absolute Discharge[3] _____
Conditional Discharge[4] _____

---

3 An absolute discharge means the offender will go free with only a written warning from the Court.
4 A conditional discharge means the offender will be released on the conditions that you, the decision-maker, set.

If the discharge were conditional, what conditions would you impose?

_____

_____

_____

Fine ___
Probation with Terms that he attends drug-counselling ___
Jail ___
I want to impose my own sentence. It is:

_____

_____

_____

TRUE LOVE

I have been living on my own since I was fourteen years old. My mother had left my father to live with another man. Her new boyfriend made it clear to me that I was not welcome to stay with them. I went to my father's house, but that did not work out either because dad was drinking a lot and bringing different women home with him almost every night. I felt awkward being in the house when the other women came, knowing they were just one of several that he had met at the bar and decided to spend the night with. I also knew dad thought I should be staying with mom.

Given that my parents didn't want me, I decided to move in with a friend, Christina. She had been living with her boyfriend who left the apartment to go back to work on the oilrigs. She was alone and looking for a roommate.

Christina was sixteen years old when I moved to her apartment. I was fourteen and turning fifteen in a few months. Christina was a good roommate and introduced me to her friends. We were having a good time because Christina liked to give parties.

We were having parties every weekend. She knew many boys who were working on the oilrigs, and when they had time off work, they came to town and wanted to party with us.

About two months after I had moved in with Christina, I met Jacob. I fell in love with him immediately. He was very popular and had his choice of all the girls in town.

I found out he liked sports, especially hockey. I knew that we had that interest in common because I was one of the best players on the girls' hockey team.

At one of the parties, Jacob noticed me and came over to talk. He mentioned that he knew my parents and asked me why I was living with Christina and not with my parents. Because he'd asked me about my personal situation, I knew it meant he cared about me.

I explained my situation to Jacob. I told him mom's new boy-friend had started coming to my room at night and was trying to get "friendly" with me. When I'd told the man to leave me alone, he became nasty to me, calling me a "stupid chick". We fought all the time and mom asked me to leave because of the fights. I couldn't go back to dads because of all the women he was bringing home. That is why I was happy when Christina asked me to move in with her.

Jacob showed me that he cared by kissing me on the cheek. He then kissed my neck and said, "You are special. You can be my little chick anytime."

Jacob stayed around me all evening. When people started get-ting ready to leave the party, he asked me if I'd like to invite him to my room. I was so happy. It was then I knew he loved me.

When he came with me to my room, he was very nice to me. He kissed and caressed me all over and politely asked if I wanted to take my shirt and pants off so he could see how beautiful I was. He did not rush me and waited for my answer. I told him I would take my clothes off, but he needed to be patient with me. I told him I had never made love before. He said we did not have to make love until I was ready and that if we decided to make love, he would be gentle with me.

Even though I was frightened, I felt comfortable with Jacob and knew he would know what to do. I let him continue to kiss and caress me. I waited for him to tell me what to do but found out that there weren't any instructions. I was surprised it was over so quickly and didn't hurt. I'd thought that it went on for longer and that I would feel more. It didn't matter because I was happy. I had made love for the first time.

I asked Jacob when I could see him again and he told me it would likely be soon because he didn't have to go back to work for another two weeks. I was so happy that I had made love and had a boyfriend. I couldn't have asked for more.

I saw Jacob twice the following week. We made love each time. I was not as nervous as the first time. He brought his ghetto blaster to my room when he visited me. Jacob told me the kind of music he liked, heavy metal. He played his music when we made love. He also told me the kind of cars he liked. He liked Mustangs. He said when he had a Mustang he would take me for a ride in it. I was ecstatic. The thought of riding through town with Jacob in his Mustang was awesome. I was certain this was true love because he was willing to share important things like music and cars with me. No one had ever shared things like that with me before.

After Jacob had gone back to work, I found out I was pregnant. I didn't have an address or a phone number for Jacob. I didn't worry about that because I believed he would come back to town when he wasn't working. I was sure Jacob would want me to have his baby so I decided to keep the baby. I waited and waited for Jacob to come back to town to see me, but he didn't come back.

I am now sixteen years old. I don't go to school anymore because I need to be with the baby.

My situation became difficult when Christina told me I needed to give her money for rent that hadn't been paid for three months. She also suggested I look for a new place to stay because having a baby in her house was cramping her style. I knew the real reason Christina wanted me to leave was because she was no longer willing to wait for me to find money for the rent. Christina also told me the reason Jacob didn't come back to see me was because he found out I was pregnant. She said he was telling people that the baby was not his and I was stupid to keep the baby.

Dad had provided money during the months I was pregnant and following the baby's birth, but he'd told me he couldn't afford to support me any more and I should find a job. I couldn't find a job because I had to care for the baby.

I realised I needed to find money to pay Christina's rent and decided it was mom's turn to help me and the baby. I thought, since the baby was her granddaughter, I should pay a call to the house where she was living and see if she would invite me back to live with her or lend me some money.

I went to the house where she was staying and knocked. A woman, whose name I later learnt was Alice, answered the door. She knew who I was and shouted to my mother, who was in the back bedroom, "Liz, your daughter, the baby factory, is here. She probably wants money from you. " I heard my mother say, "Tell her to go away. She should have kept her legs closed."

I tried to push past Alice, but she had braced her arms in front of me and pushed me back. I told her to "let me through, I just want to talk to my mother. I want to tell her about her new granddaughter."

Alice kept trying to push me away, but I shoved her aside and kept going towards the bedroom where my mother was. When I got to the bedroom, I saw mom was still in bed.

"What do you want?" she said. "I'm not giving you money if that's what you came for."

I heard voices in the kitchen where Alice was. I heard Alice's voice and the voice of a man. I heart Alice say "She's in the back bedroom with her mother. She wouldn't leave when I told her to leave; she pushed me aside to get in."

I stood listening to hear more of the conversation. I wanted to find out what the man was saying.

I didn't have a chance to tell mom anything before a police officer came into the room. His first question was to my mother, "Are you alright, Mrs Trace? Is your daughter visiting you"? My mother's response to his question was, "No, I didn't invite her here. I don't want her around. I told her to go away."

My heart fell. How could my mother say this?

The officer looked over at me and motioned for me to step outside with him. We left the house together and once outside he instructed me to take a seat in the back of his police car. I did as he said. There was another officer in the car, so I waited with the second officer while the first officer went back into the house to speak to Alice and my mother.

When the first officer came back to the car, he said, "Miss Trace, I am sorry, but I have to charge you with an offence because you did not have the right to be at the house after you had been asked to leave by both Mrs Stacks and your mother. You had no right to push Mrs Stacks aside in order to get into the house."

I started to cry when I heard he was going to charge me with criminal offences. I couldn't believe what Alice and my mother must have told him. My mother must really hate me!

The officer continued speaking, "Miss Trace, I could charge you with trespassing because Mrs Stacks asked you to leave. However, given that I think you have learnt a lesson that you cannot burst into someone's house without invitation, I will give you a break and only charge you with assault for pushing Mrs Stacks."

I couldn't believe my bad luck. The visit to talk to my mother and to see if she would invite me back to live with her or loan me some money resulted in being charged with a criminal offence.

If I hadn't had the baby, I would have entered a guilty plea and gone to prison. At least it would have given me a place to stay. I couldn't do that, however, because I had to look after my baby.

I entered a plea of not guilty and went to trial. I had a student lawyer from Torcia's Student Assistance Programme help me at the trial.

Alice Stacks and my mother both gave evidence against me. It hurt me so much to hear my mother say that I only came to get money from her.

The Torcia State lawyer asked me in cross-examination why I had gone to the house that day. I didn't tell the truth. I told the Court I only wanted to talk to my mother about my baby. It was painful to admit I needed money and I'd hoped mom would invite me to come back to stay with her.

I was convicted of assault.

The judge asked why the baby's father was not helping pay to look after the baby. She also asked if I had anything to say about the sentence to be imposed.

I was too shy to speak to the judge but asked the student lawyer to tell the judge that I had no contact with the baby's father although I'd heard he'd been sent to jail for stealing a car. I also asked her to tell the judge that I'd found a place to stay, a big house where I would live with six people and do the cooking and cleaning in order to pay for my rent.

The sentence the judge gave me was a conditional discharge. I am to report to a probation officer and keep the peace and be of good behaviour for a period of one year. I am not to go within five hundred yards of my mother's residence during that time.

What I really wanted to tell the judge but did not have the courage to say was the important lesson I'd learnt. This was not "true love."

The Judgement Game
1) What social problems are addressed in the vignette *True Love?*

_____

_____

_____

2) Do you agree with the Trial Court decision?

Yes ☐

No ☐

If you do not agree with the Trial Court decision, what punishment would you impose?

Absolute Discharge [5]____

Conditional Discharge[6] _____

If the discharge were conditional, what conditions would you impose?

_____

_____

_____

Fine ____

Probation with terms that the offender takes counselling for violence. ____

Jail ____

I want to impose my own sentence. It is:

_____

_____

5 An absolute discharge means the offender will go free with only a written warning.
6 A conditional discharge means the offender will go free on conditions that you, the decision maker, set.

Self-Assessment

You have the opportunity to provide a self-assessment after reading the vignettes in "Family Affairs."

Indicate how many points* you give yourself for:

1) Recognition of issues raised in the chapter. ___
2) Suggestions and comments you made. ___
3) Your role as a decision maker. ___
TOTAL: ___

*You can give yourself 0 (lowest) to 5 (highest) points.
This is a game. Remember there are no right or wrong answers.

CHAPTER 3:
ADDICTIONS AND OBSESSIONS

• • •

You are the sentencing decision maker. In each case, a crime has been committed. You read a summary of the evidence given to the Trial Court. In addition to providing a sentence, you are asked: Does the offender have an addiction or an obsession?

You will play *The Judgement Game* in each case by using your own judgement to choose one of the sentences provided.

ROSES FOR VICKY

The offender, did not give evidence
Evidence of Vicky

I'm a financial advisor with a banking firm. I work on the twenty-ninth floor of an office building. My office handles a great deal of confidential bank information for the State that necessitates a high level of security. Because of the high security, I had to sign in at the security desk when going to work, when leaving work, and each time I would come or go from the office.

Three weeks after I started work with my firm, a bouquet of roses arrived at my house. There was a card with the bouquet, "From your secret admirer." I did not know from whom the roses had been sent. They were beautiful and I placed them in a vase in my dining room.

Another bouquet of roses arrived the following week with the same message. I again placed the flowers in a vase in my dining room. I wondered if my secret admirer was a client or a person from my office.

A few weeks later, I received a letter in my mailbox. The card inside the envelope contained a handwritten message that said, "I adore you. From your secret admirer."

I was confused by what was happening. I had no boyfriend. I had no potential boyfriends. I wondered if some of the male advisors in my office were sending me these messages as a joke. I also wondered if it might be a female. I am not a lesbian and I have no experiences with women. I started to become paranoid and to watch everyone around me to see if I could figure out who was sending these messages and who my secret admirer was.

Another card arrived. This time the words on the card said, "Be Mine." I didn't know what to do. I thought if I ignored the messages, he or she would stop sending them. I threw the card in the garbage.

An unusual event occurred about the same time. One night when I was working at my office, I received a call from the security office. The officer said "You are the only person in the building. You must leave the building because there has been a fire reported on the eleventh floor and we need to let the firemen deal with the problem." The officer said, "Don't take the elevator. I will come to the twenty-ninth floor to escort you down the emergency stairs."

The call bothered me because I was in the middle of completing a report for my office but had no choice but to stop my work and wait for the security officer to arrive. It was not long before the officer arrived at my office door. He was a small man but his physique suggested he was into muscle building.

I got up from my chair and asked him what I had to do. He told me that he would walk down the twenty-nine flights of stairs with me. He said people often experienced vertigo because of the steep steps and narrow staircase. The mere thought of descending that number of flights made me queasy. It did not help that I knew I was alone with this man because he said I was the only person in the building. The officer told me to go ahead of him and not to take anything with me except my car keys because I would not be able to return to my office that evening.

As we descended the stairs, he followed close behind me. I could feel his breath, but I did not turn around. He smelled strongly of some kind of men's cologne. I just walked ahead of him.

I was wearing high heels, which made it difficult to keep my balance as I was going down the steps. Once or twice when I stumbled, the guard reached out to help me keep my balance.

When we arrived at the bottom of the stairs, I did not see any fire engines outside the building or any fire fighters in the building. I was tired and just wanted a drink of water. I mentioned that to him and he went to the security office and brought me back a bottle of water. The man was doing his job and trying to protect me so I tried to be nice to him although I realized I would not be able to go back to finish my work that evening.

The next day I told people at my office of the event. No one had heard of a problem on the eleventh floor. I assumed the problem had not been serious and I did not think any more about it.

I went back and forth to work as usual for the next few weeks. There were no more flowers or messages. I thought my secret admirer must have had a short infatuation, and I was pleased, as he or she had been starting to scare me.

Two months later, a neighbour stopped me when I arrived home. The lady, a friendly woman, asked me if I had instructed someone to pick up my mail. I asked her why she was asking me that question and she replied that she and her husband had seen a man going past my house each day and looking into my mailbox. I told the neighbour I had not instructed anyone to pick up my mail. I could not figure this out, as I believed I was receiving all my mail.

Not long after that I realised I did have a problem. I had been coming home each night at about seven o'clock. It was my routine to eat dinner, watch the local and international news, and then go to bed. One night as I was preparing dinner, I heard a dog barking and looked out my window. When I looked out, I saw a figure standing on the sidewalk beside my bedroom window. I could not see the person clearly, as it was getting dark, but it frightened me to think that someone was looking into my bedroom window. I finished dinner and stayed up for awhile watching television. I could not sleep, however, as I kept wondering who had been outside my house.

The next day I told a friend at my office about the figure outside my window. I also told her about the flowers and messages I had been receiving. She suggested I call the police. She said it appeared that someone was stalking me. I did not do anything at that time because I thought her idea far-fetched and paranoid.

About one month later, the next message arrived: "I need you." The words of this message were not handwritten like the others but were cut from a newspaper and pasted on a card. That is when I decided I had better call the police. It seemed more serious to receive an anonymous message cut from a newspaper rather than one handwritten. This message scared me.

I gave the police the card I had received and told them about the other messages and unusual things that had been happening to me. I told them about the flowers and cards, the mailbox, and the figure who had been standing outside my bedroom window. They asked me if I had kept any of the other cards or the wrapping paper for the flowers I had previously received. I told them I had thrown everything out. They said that would make it difficult for them to trace the sender but they would start a report with the information I had just given them. The police opened a file regarding my complaint and told me to call them if anything more happened.

Within days, the next event happened. I received an envelope containing several loose photographs. The photographs were of me at my office, at the grocery store and shopping for clothes. I was totally unnerved. My privacy had been invaded. I called the police immediately. I was now very frightened to be at home alone. I did not want to go anywhere except my office, where I felt safe.

I contacted the police and gave them the envelope with the photographs. When the police officer looked at the photographs, she said there were no markings to show where the photographs had been developed and she suspected the photos had been developed by the sender himself or herself. She said the letter gave a postmark, which would help the police with the investigation. The officer took the information and said she or someone from the police would be in touch with me.

I waited three weeks before I heard from the police again. I'd been living in fear wondering if I would ever be free to live my life without being followed. An officer called and asked me to attend the police office as a suspect had been arrested in relation to my case. I breathed a sigh of relief and was eager to find out who had been arrested.

When I arrived at the police station, I was told that security personnel at my local supermarket had contacted the police to report an incident of theft. Apparently, a man tried to leave the supermarket without paying for a fitness magazine. When the security officer stopped the man and confiscated the magazine, the officer found loose photographs, similar to the ones I had received in the post, placed in the magazine. The police showed me the photos that had been confiscated. There were photographs of me checking in and out at the security desk of my office, photos of me shopping and photos of me undressing as I was getting ready for bed. My God, this creep was obsessed with me. It made me shutter. This person had been following me.

The police said that when they laid criminal charges against the man, he said:

"Don't let them take my job away. I watch her day and night. She is mine. My job is to keep her safe."

The Judgement Game
Do you feel that the man who stole the fitness magazine had an addiction or an obsession?

Yes ☐ No ☐

What Sentence Would You Impose?
1) A six-month order against the man that is reviewable every thirty days prohibiting him from having any contact with Vicky. The man must enrol in a one-year programme to deal with obsessive behaviour. The State will pay for this programme.

Yes ☐ No ☐

2) The man cannot be changed. He will go to jail for one year.

Yes ☐ No ☐

3) The man should be charged with Stalking. [7]

Yes ☐ No ☐

4) The man has a psychiatric problem. He should be sent to a psychiatric centre for an indefinite period, to be released when the centre determines he has dealt with his obsessive behaviour.

Yes ☐ No ☐

---

7 Stalking is one of Torcia's criminal offences. (See Annex B) Psychologists and psychiatrists in Torcia have become aware of the problem of stalking and are working with offenders who exhibit this type of obsessive behaviour. Criminal Courts in Torcia are aware that it requires the Court's attention in dealing with offenders who exhibit this type of behaviour. How the Court will, deal with people convicted of stalking will be a decision for each judge to make depending on the circumstances of the offence, the offender and the victim. There is no mandatory sentence or period of incarceration for this offence. The offence carries a maximum period of imprisonment of ten years.

5) The community should sentence the offender, not the State.

Yes ☐ No ☐

6) I want to create my own sentence. It is:

_____

_____

_____

7) Do you feel that seeing the man who stole the magazine might have had an impact on your sentence?

Yes ☐ No ☐

Why or why not?

_____

_____

_____

BEWARE OF BETTY

Betty is charged with assault causing bodily harm. The victim, Greg Dodsworth, is a young man who visited her property on business. He was working for the gas line department and needed her to sign a document to allow State workers to enter her property to install gas lines.

Dodsworth´s evidence

The day I called at Betty Fabien´s house, I saw signs indicating it was a private home and that a dangerous dog guarded the premises. Because of the sign, I sounded my horn when I approached the house and did not immediately get out of my vehicle but waited for someone to come out of the house.

A woman carrying a rifle came out of the house. I did not reverse my truck and leave, but waited until she was within hearing distance and rolled down my window to announce who I was and the purpose of my visit. She acted as if I had interrupted her and said that she was on her way to shoot gophers when she heard me drive in. That explained why she had the gun, but I was still somewhat surprised by her manner.

She said she had received a letter from the gas line department to say the State would be installing gas lines on her property and that a representative would be contacting her. She said, "You must be the representative."

Ms Fabien went on to say she could not understand why the State had chosen her property for the gas lines. Her words were, "Why can't they leave anything alone? Why do they have to destroy the environment and use my property to do it"?

I decided not to respond to her comment, but to proceed with my job. I knew that workers from my department were scheduled to attend her property the following week to install the gas lines.

I needed to advise her where the lines were to be installed, the payment she would be receiving for an easement to cross her land, and to obtain her signature to allow my department to apply for the easement. Her manner was cool, but she nodded her head affirmatively when I asked if she would sign the paper authorising the workers to cross her property to install the gas lines. "I'll sign the bloody paper, but I want to give you a piece of my mind about the mess and damage it will cause to my property."

She told me her dog was in the house and it was safe for me to get out of the truck and go to the house so she could review and sign the papers. I got out of the truck and followed her. We went up a few steps at the entrance to the house so she could open the door. When she opened the door, a dog came bounding out and grabbed me by the arm, sinking its teeth into my flesh. Ms Fabien immediately spun around when the dog attacked me and hit me in the face with the rifle she was carrying. She did not do anything to call the dog off, although I was shouting and screaming in pain. I managed to kick the dog and get him to lessen his grip on my arm so I could get away. Once I was free, I immediately ran back to my truck.

I saw that my arm was bleeding and I realised that I needed medical assistance. My nose was throbbing and I believed it was broken. I was able to use my cellular phone to call my office. Ms Fabien did not try to follow me to the truck or assist me.

I drove to the hospital, about half an hour away from the Fabien property. I went to emergency where my injuries were treated. The doctor gave me a tetanus shot and fifteen stitches to my arm. I found out from the doctor that my nose was broken. He said there was nothing I could do except to let it heal. He pre-scribed painkillers for me and told me that my nose will always be crooked.

I took two weeks off work to recover from the incident. I had to return to the hospital to have my arm checked and the stitches removed.

Betty Fabien's evidence

The warning signs were clear. He had no right to enter my property. I had been going out to shoot gophers when the man arrived. He did not announce his arrival, although I saw he was driving a State vehicle. He got out of his truck and approached the front door of my house. My dog, Rico, was outside the house where he had been waiting to go with me to shoot gophers. Wanting to ensure I would be protected, Rico ran towards the man who had exited his vehicle and was approaching the house. Rico grabbed the man by the arm. When I saw the man struggling with Rico. I rushed towards them with the gun I was carrying and waved it at Rico to stop him from attacking the man. The barrel of the gun hit the man by mistake, although I was trying to hit Rico.

The Court's Decision Prior to Sentencing
I find Betty Fabien guilty of assault causing bodily harm. I have taken a special interest in this case and have obtained a pre-sentence report to shed light on what I describe as an unwarranted assault on the victim, Mr Dodsworth. I have sought information to show me why the accused acted in the manner she did during this incident. From information that Ms Fabien provided to the social worker who prepared the pre-sentence report, I learnt that Ms Fabien has a desire for seclusion and wants to live in a place where she can withdraw from people. She did everything she could to ensure that people were not welcome to enter her property. She erected gates and barriers to indicate that no one should enter. The signs were clear: "Do Not Enter, Private Property, Dangerous Dog."

When people, such as Mr Dodsworth, needed to enter her property to deal with commercial matters, they are made to feel uncomfortable. The gun that she had with her that day, allegedly for hunting gophers, should not have been used in the way it was used. It is a dangerous weapon. The butt of the rifle hit Mr Dodsworth squarely in the face. I do not accept her evidence that she was trying to hit the dog.

Ms Fabien has no immediate family or children. Her dog is her friend. The venom she carries for people causes me to shiver. Ms Fabien told the social worker she would like to have been born in a different era, an era prior to the invention of motor vehicles and modern technology. She told the social worker that she just wants to be left alone with her animals. She told the social worker, "animals are my friends, not people."

The Judgement Game
Do you feel Ms Fabien has an addiction or an obsession?
Yes [ ] No [ ]

What Sentence Would You Impose?

1) A six-month order against Ms Fabien that is reviewable every thirty days prohibiting her from having any contact with Mr Dodsworth. Ms Fabien must enrol in a one-year programme to deal with obsessive behaviour. The State will pay for this programme.
Yes [   ] No [   ]

2) Ms Fabien cannot be changed. She will go to jail for one year.
Yes [   ] No [   ]

3) Ms. Fabien should be charged with Stalking. See Annex B for Torcia's Stalking law.
Yes [   ] No [   ]

Why or Why Not?

_____

_____

_____

4) Ms Fabien has a psychiatric problem. She should be sent to a psychiatric centre for an indefinite period, to be released when the centre determines she has dealt with her obsessive behaviour.
Yes [   ] No [   ]

5) The community should sentence Ms Fabien, not the State.
Yes [   ] No [   ]

6) I want to create my own sentence. It is:

_____

_____

_____

7) Do you feel that seeing Betty Fabien might have had an impact on your sentence?
Yes [   ] No [   ]

Why or why not?

_____

_____

_____

REG´S REPENTENCE

Reg is charged with assault causing bodily harm. He entered a guilty plea to the charge.

Torcia State lawyer's Sentencing Submission

The present charge arises from an incident where the victim and accused were drinking at Woody's Bar in Jervis. The victim was hit in the face by the accused. The victim suffered a broken nose.

When the police arrived at the scene, the offender acknowledged that he had hit the victim. The police report indicates it appeared the offender assaulted the victim without provocation. The offender was arrested without incident. The victim advised that he had been trying to jokes with the offender when the offender assaulted him.

The offender has a previous record for assaults. There are four previous convictions of assault, all involving bar room incidents.

The State acknowledges that the offender is mentally challenged. This may explain his actions, however, no evidence has been provided to the Court to show Reg did not have the ability to understand his actions.

Reg´s Lawyer's Sentencing Submission

Reg is fifty years old. He is not working and lives alone. He has entered a guilty plea at the first opportunity.

In the present situation, the man who Reg assaulted had been making jokes at the bar and had used Reg´s name in his jokes. Reg advises he thought the man was making fun of him and immediately punched the man in the nose. Reg advised that he gets angry when he believes people are making fun of him. Reg says this has happened before.

Reg acknowledges that the victim's nose was broken. It is submitted that Reg´s action of striking the victim was spontaneous and without forethought.

Reg expresses his remorse for the offence. He wishes to make an apology to the victim and has written a letter of apology that I have provided to the Torcia State lawyer to give to the victim.

```
I´S SORI MR.
FRUM
REG
```

The Judgement Game
Do you feel Reg had any addiction or has exhibited obsessive behaviour?
Yes [ ] No [ ]

What sentence would you impose?
1) A six-month order against Reg that is reviewable every thirty days prohibiting her from having any contact with the victim. Reg must enrol in a one-year programme to deal with obsessive behaviour. The State will pay for this programme.
Yes [ ] No [ ]

2) Reg cannot be changed. He will go to jail for one year.
Yes [ ] No [ ]

3) Reg should be charged with Stalking. * See Annex B for Torcia´s Stalking law.
Yes ☐ No ☐

4) Reg has a psychiatric problem. He should be sent to a psychiatric centre for an indefinite period, to be released when the centre determines he has dealt with his obsessive behaviour.
Yes ☐ No ☐

5) The community should sentence Reg, not the State.
Yes ☐ No ☐

6) I want to create my own sentence. It is:

_____

_____

_____

7) Do you feel that seeing Reg might have had an impact on your sentence?
Yes ☐ No ☐

Why or why not?

_____

_____

_____

DARLENE´S DILEMMA

This is the third time I have been convicted of theft. I could afford to pay for the things that I stole, but something always stops me from paying when I leave the store.

The first time I was convicted, I was given a conditional discharge. The decision maker just wanted me to keep the peace and bc of good behaviour for a period of six months. The second time I had to reimburse the store for the item I had stolen. This time, you have said that it appears I had not learnt my lesson and the sentence you give me must make an impact on me so I will stop stealing these items. On each occasion, I have stolen a package of condoms. After my conviction, you asked me if I had anything to say.

This is what I have to say:

I was twelve years old when mom told me to make sure I never came home with a baby. She said, "Make sure you don't get knocked up, girl."

At that time, I didn't understand what getting knocked up meant but realised it had something to do with letting men get into your trousers. Mom told me men are all the same. She said, "You watch out. It won't be long now and you'll find out! Men are the same; all they want to do is get into your trousers."

I didn't see any men trying to get into my trousers, but I started watching them to make sure they didn't touch my trousers.

I have two brothers and a sister. My brothers are both older than I am. They spent most of their time with dad and left me in the house with mom. Dad took the boys with him to work in the fields, but I had to stay in the house to help mom with the cooking and cleaning. I learnt how to clean the house and how to make pies and cakes.

My sister was killed when she was three years old. She had been playing in the driveway and was run over by a truck. The driver hadn't seen her when he was backing up. I was six years old when it happened. My twin brothers were ten years old. Everyone told me Mom changed after my sister's death. I don't think so. I think mom was always crazy.

Mom tried to kill me when I was ten years old. She took a knife and held it to my throat. "You are an evil child," she screamed. "You are the one who should have died, not your sister." One of my brothers who came running into the kitchen when he heard me screaming saved me. I was lucky he was in the house when this happened. He was fourteen and was used to mom's tantrums. He was calm with her. He told her to let me go and that he would look after punishing me for upsetting her. She let me go.

I also read a lot to escape mom's incessant blabbering. I had heard her story often. She told me:

"I didn't want to have babies but men are all the same, all they want to do is get into your trousers. Your twin brothers were the first, then you, and then your sister. He wanted more, but I aborted the last one and almost died from the bleeding. The bleeding finally stopped, but I knew I could not have more children."

To avoid listening to mom's stories, I created plays. I used my dolls in the plays. I created different characters for each of my dolls. When I didn't like a doll, I would cut off her hair. I would also paint her private parts with bright splashes of red or dark black marks. That doll would get all of the bad parts in the plays. The cute round dolls were the ones I didn't like, the ones that looked like babies. I wanted adult-looking dolls. Dark ones or blonde ones were fine, but they needed to look like adults. They needed to be slim and tall. They needed long legs. They could not be cute or chubby. They could have breasts, but their breasts could not be too big.

I didn't want ordinary dolls. I wanted adult dolls. I wanted dolls I could talk to.

I didn't have any boy dolls. I wanted some but was never given any. I had to play with girl dolls until I was older and could find my own boy dolls.

It was when I started playing with my first boy doll that things went wrong. I didn't follow mom's instructions and let him get into my trousers. I knew I could not bring babies home. I decided the only thing I could do was to have an abortion.

I knew I could not let it happen again. That is when I started stealing condoms.

That is what I have to say.

The Judgement Game

Do you feel Darlene had an addiction or an obsession?

Yes [ ] No [ ]

What Sentence Would You Impose?

1) Darlene cannot be changed. She will go to jail for one year.

Yes [ ] No [ ]

2) Darlene has a psychiatric problem. She should be sent to a psychiatric centre for an indefinite period, to be released when the centre determines she has dealt with her obsessive behaviour.

Yes [ ] No [ ]

3) The community should sentence Darlene, not the State.

Yes [ ] No [ ]

4) I want to create my own sentence. It is:

_____

_____

_____

5) Do you feel that seeing Darlene might have had an impact on your sentence?

Yes [ ] No [ ]

Why or why not?

_____

_____

_____

Self-Assessment

You have the opportunity to provide a self-assessment after reading the vignettes in "Addictions and Obsessions."

Indicate how many points* you give yourself for:

1) Recognition of issues raised in the chapter. ___

2) Suggestions and comments you made. ___

3) Your role as a decision maker. ___

TOTAL: ___

*You can give yourself 0 (lowest) to 5 (highest) points.

This is a game. Remember there are no right or wrong answers.

CHAPTER 4:
THE OMNIPOTENT DECISION MAKER

• • •

In this chapter, you are the omnipotent decision maker. You will see the face of the offender in different ways and from different perspectives. You will be given information by the offender, including discussions between the offender and his or her legal counsel, as well as information provided by third parties such as social workers and psychologists. You will be given information that would normally not be disclosed to a judge because of solicitor/client privilege. This allows you, the omnipotent decision maker, to have a more complete understanding of the offence and the offender.

In some of the reports, you are given only basic comments about the offence and the offender. In these cases, you will be asked what additional information you feel you require to make a judgement about the sentence to be imposed.

Remember, there are no right and wrong answers. The sentence imposed is your decision.

TONY´S TROUBLE

Tony's Meeting with his Lawyer
I know I am in a shitload of trouble this time. The pigs "went to town" with the charges they laid against me: driving without a licence, impaired driving, reckless driving causing death.

Holy shit! I was only driving across the city to get to a different bar when the accident happened. I feel bad about the woman and child who were killed, but you know, shit happens.

It isn't worth trying to fight the charges. I know I will be sent back to jail. That's why I'm here to see you today. I might as well start the ball rolling and get this over with. You can go ahead and plead me guilty.

I don't have any money, but I know you'll be able to get the Torcia Legal Assistance Programme to pay for my case. You've done that before.

I had no driver's license because it had been taken from me the last time I was in Court.

Court Appearance
After discussions between Tony's lawyer and the Torcia State lawyer, Tony agreed to enter guilty pleas to two charges. The State dropped the charge of impaired driving.
Tony Entered Guilty Pleas To:
- Reckless Driving Causing Death
- Driving Without a Licence

Submissions to the Court by Torcia State's Lawyer
Tony Borris is a threat to society. His record shows he has been convicted of impaired driving and driving without a licence on several previous occasions. He has been fined, placed on probation, and sent to jail. Nothing works to stop him from continuing to wreak havoc on Torcia's roads and highways. I ask that you send him to jail for a lengthy period. I submit that five years, consecutive, is appropriate for each charge. I also ask that you recommend to the Torcia Driver Registry that it impose a lifetime prohibition on this man from ever obtaining a licence.

I have spoken with Mr Borris' counsel and he acknowledges Mr Borris' criminal record, which shows:

- Four previous convictions of impaired driving
- Three convictions for driving without a licence

Submissions to the Court by Tony's Lawyer

Tony Borris is pleading guilty at the first opportunity.

Tony is fifty-nine years of age. He is divorced and has lived in Wella all of his life. He doesn't have any children. Tony works as a casual labourer.

Tony has asked me to express his remorse for the accident and the death of the other driver and her daughter.

It is submitted that two-year sentences, concurrent would be appropriate for the two charges for which Tony has entered guilty pleas.

Trial Court Decision

For the reckless driving causing death charge, you will spend thirty-six months in jail and be given a five-year licence suspension.

For the driving without a licence, you are sentenced to a period of twelve months in jail and given a two-year licence suspension.

These sentences are consecutive, meaning that you will serve one after the other.

Mr Borris, this is not a joke. A woman and her child lost their lives because you were drinking and driving. You must wake up to what you have done and the danger you cause others. I am sentencing you to a significant period in jail. I cannot cure your sickness, and I believe it is a sickness, but I want to tell you clearly that you need help. You must do something to address your drinking problem.

Tony's Comments to His Lawyer Following Sentence

I don't need a lecture from that old coot! Torcia is a free country, he can't tell me what to do. I can drink if I want to.

It's bullshit if the judge thinks he is going to stop me from driving when I get out of jail! Everyone knows that driving is a fundamental right in Torcia. I've been driving since I was five years old.

I know when I am in prison they'll make me go to courses to try to stop me from drinking. That is just a waste of time and money. I have taken those courses before, but they don't work. I find as much to drink when I'm in jail as when I'm on the street.

I am not an alcoholic. I just enjoy drinking.

The Judgement Game

1) Would you uphold the Trial Court decision?

Yes ☐ No ☐

2) What sentencing principle or principles do you believe the Court used when sentencing Tony? (See Annex A)

_____

_____

_____

3) Do you feel that the information provided to you, the omnipotent decision maker, made a difference to your understanding of this vignette?

Yes ☐ No ☐

Why or why not?

_____

_____

_____

4) Do you feel it would have made a different decision if you had been able to see and speak to Tony?

Yes ☐ No ☐

Why or why not?

_____

_____

_____

MATTHEW'S PLEA

The State of Torcia has appealed the sentence of the Trial Court for impaired driving that gave Matthew an AA Discharge to take training to deal with his alcohol problem. The state had previously supported the sentence awarded by the Trial Court, but after a senior legal counsel from the Torcia State Justice Department looked at Matthew's previous record and list of convictions, he decided the department should appeal the Trial Court decision.

You are the sole decision maker of the Court of Appeal. You are asked to make the decision for this appeal. You can either leave the trial judge's decision in place or award a different sentence for Matthew's two offences: impaired driving and driving with excessive speed.

Matthew's lawyer made submissions to the judge at the Trial Court. For this appeal, Matthew makes his own written submission to you.

Matthew's Submission

I want to tell you about my problem with alcohol abuse. I also want to tell you how I was able to resolve my problem.

My name is Matthew Cahill. The police stopped me because I had been speeding. The bad news was that I'd been drinking and the police officer could smell the whiskey on my breath. He asked me to attend at the police station and blow into a Breathalyzer machine. Unfortunately, I failed the test. This is the same problem I'd dealt with before, impaired driving. This time there is another charge as well, driving with excessive speed.

My criminal record is bad. It has been a few years since I was caught, but it happened again. The last time was terrible. I killed a person, an elderly man. I have tried to block this incident out of my mind to keep myself sane. I've tried to forget the memory, but I can't. It has come back to haunt me. I want to stop the thoughts, but they won't go away. I keep having flashbacks of the accident.

I see the blur of oncoming lights. My foot hits the brake. There is a squeal of tires. There is a howling sound of metal hitting metal. Something sharp hits me. I feel pain across my forehead. I can't breathe. I'm bleeding. I can taste the blood, sweet and sticky against my lips. I can't move. My hands are gripping the steering wheel.

Everything goes black.

I hear voices saying, "That's the driver who hit the other car head on. The man didn't have a chance. He died before...."

I was charged with Reckless Driving Causing Death and Impaired Driving. I went to Court. I entered guilty pleas and was sent to jail. I kept my head down and did my time. I found lots of booze in jail. We'd often make our own.

When I got out of jail, I tried to stop drinking but I couldn't. I am a plumber and I drank almost every day after work and sometimes, when I was working on my own, I drank when I was on the job.

On this occasion, I was driving home after finishing a plumbing job where I had been drinking all afternoon. I was stopped for speeding.

The police officer who stopped me told me I had the right to contact a lawyer. I called a lawyer from the list of lawyers he gave me. I spoke with a lawyer who said he would stop by the police station to see me that afternoon.

When the lawyer arrived at the station, an officer brought him to the lawyer interview room. I wanted a whiskey to give me strength but knew I couldn't have one. I was lucky the police station had a coffee machine and I bought myself a coffee. I recall trying to concentrate on drinking the coffee, but the smell of coffee combined with my perspiration was making me sick. On the other hand, perhaps it was the fear of recognising who I was and what I had done that was making me sick. The cup I was gripping was a crutch for me to hold when I talked to the lawyer.

I told him I wanted to plead guilty. I told him about the accident when I killed a man and the flashbacks I was having of that accident. I told him that alcohol was destroying me and I couldn't forget what I had done.

I told the lawyer about my previous convictions. In the last five years, I'd been convicted of:

Theft over $1000;

Impaired Driving and Driving without a Licence;

Impaired Driving and three convictions of Driving without a Licence,

Reckless Driving Causing Death

Given my record, I asked the lawyer how long I was likely to be in jail this time. He interrupted me. I remember his words: "Mr Cahill, slow down. I have several clients with stories and records similar to yours. What I need to know is, do you want to deal with your drinking problem? If you do, there are people who can help you."

I believe it was his words, "There are people who can help you," that caused me to break down. I started to sob like a baby. His cold manner and formality was a stark contrast to his words. Finally, I had reason to believe there might be hope for me.

Our second meeting was at his office. He explained the law he would use to help me. He told me he had already spoken with the lawyer for the State of Torcia about my case. He said the Torcia State lawyer was willing to entertain his application to the Trial Court for what he called, an "AA discharge". I tried to understand what he was telling me, but it was over my head. What I knew is that I had to see a doctor, and would have to take treatment and counselling. From what he said, it sounded like I would be going to "boot camp."

This is the legal provision he showed me and that he provided to the Trial Court:

(AA=Alcohol Addiction)

AADischarge, Section 942:

When a person has committed the offence of impaired driving, a Court may make an order, called an AA Discharge. Rather than imposing normal legal penalties for the offence of impaired driving, an AA Discharge can be made when the offender presents medical or other evidence to show he is in need of treatment to overcome his addiction to alcohol, and it is shown to the Court that the public of Torcia would benefit from treating the offender's addiction. Where an AA Discharge is made, the Court will make an AA Order setting out conditions for treatment of the offender for a specified period.

I don't understand this legal gobbledygook, but my lawyer, the State lawyer, and the judge all seemed to understand. I've given you a copy of the section he gave me so you can see what my lawyer gave the judge.

When we attended Court, my lawyer made his submissions and provided medical evidence from my doctor showing I was ill and outlining the steps I had taken to deal with my alcohol addiction. Reports from social workers and my doctor were given to the judge. Information was also provided of my attendance at the Torcia Treatment Centre (TTC), or as I called it, "boot camp." It had been tough. They were very strict.

The judge granted my lawyer's application for the AA Discharge for a two-year period based on the fact I had satisfied the judge that I had stopped drinking. The judge set out conditions in an AA Order. One of the conditions was that I must meet with AA officers every week for the two-year period.

Following Court, I received a letter from my lawyer explaining what happened. I provide a copy of that letter for you and hope it will convince you to keep the Trial Court's sentence in place so I can complete my sentence.

Dear Mr Cahill:

I confirm my attendance for you in the Court of Torcia on Monday, June 4th. At that, time evidence of your attendance with the alcohol treatment staff of Torcia Treatment Centre (TTC) was introduced to the Court. Joint representations were made by my office and the Torcia State Lawyer with respect to the sentence for the offences for which you entered guilty pleas, impaired driving and a driving with excessive speed.

The Court awarded an AA Discharge for a term of two years on the terms set out in the order that you signed at the Clerk's office. The judge reviewed the terms of the AA Order for you in Court, and a copy of the terms was provided to you. The terms are extensive and require your review and compliance with them for the two-year period. You must continue your treatment during that time as specified in the Order.

The Court also ordered a mandatory driving suspension for a period of one year, emphasising that you are not to drive any form of motor vehicle during that time. The Court gave you three months to pay the traffic ticket for driving with excessive speed, being a fine of $1,000.

Thank you for requesting my representation. I wish you continued success in your endeavours.

Yours truly,
Your lawyer

B. Goode

The Judgement Game

1) Would you uphold the Trial Decision to give Matthew an AA Discharge under Section 942?

Yes ☐ No ☐

2) Do you believe the AA Discharge provision can be used for <u>all</u> <u>offenders</u> who have committed offences of impaired driving?

_____

_____

_____

Why or why not?

_____

_____

_____

3) Do you feel it would have made a difference to your decision if you had been able to see and speak to Matthew?

Yes [   ] No [   ]

Why or why not?

_____

_____

_____

RECIDIVISM AND LIES: A REVOLVING DOOR

Jack is a lawyer in Torcia. Jack's clients include the Flintrock family. From generation to generation, the Flintrock family has required legal services for crimes such as drug, alcohol, theft and assault offences. The Flintrock family are petty thieves and drug offenders. Fred, their patriarch, has a lengthy record for impaired driving offences, theft, and soft drug offences. Most of his offences resulted in guilty pleas or plea-bargains that Jack arranged for him.

The latest offences Jack was asked to handle were two charges against Fred's nephew, Jim. They were charges of uttering a death threat and assault. Jim is eighteen years old and works in the construction industry where he helps with site excavations.

Following review of the case, Jack decided to take the matters to trial.

Jim's information to Jack prior to trial.

I went to my trailer to talk to my sister's boyfriend Alex. My sister Tracy had called me earlier in the week and told me that Alex had assaulted her when he was drunk. I wanted to have a word with him and let him know that I would call the police if I heard he hurt my sister again.

Tracy told me that Alex was sleeping as he had been up all night drinking with his friends. She said that I should come back when he was awake. I looked at my watch and it was four o'clock in the afternoon. I decided to wake him.

When I opened the bedroom door, I saw Alex was already up. I didn't have a chance to say or do anything. Alex met me with a baseball bat in his hands. My first response was to hit him before he hit me. I did not have a chance to say anything to him.

Jack reviewed Jim's criminal record with him prior to trial. Jim acknowledged that he had been convicted of the offences shown in the police disclosure report, being two previous convictions for assault causing bodily harm within the past two years and four convictions for possession of marijuana and one conviction for possession of cocaine, all having taken place in the past three years.

The First Trial

Jim's trial was started on a previous occasion but was adjourned because one witness, Alex, failed to appear. The Court rescheduled the trial. The Court told the Torcia State lawyer to ensure he provided subpoenas to all of the State's witnesses.

The Torcia State lawyer served subpoenas on its witnesses, Alex and Tracy.

The Second Trial

Tracy attended Court and gave evidence. Alex did not come to Court. The State did not apply for a further adjournment, as the Torcia State lawyer knew the Court would be unlikely to grant a further adjournment.

Tracy's evidence

Examination-in-Chief:

My brother Jim came to the trailer that I was renting from him. He told me that Alex owed him money for a car that Jim had sold him. He was swearing and shouting at Alex, "I'm going to kill you, you bastard! I want my money." He pushed his way past me still shouting. "Alex, you Fuck, I am going to kill you"! The next thing I heard was a scream and saw Alex coming out of the bedroom with a bloody nose.

Tracy attempted to enter a blood stained t-shirt, which she said Alex had been wearing the day of the incident. The Trial Judge refused to allow the t-shirt to be entered as an exhibit for lack of proof that it was Alex's t-shirt or that the blood on the t-shirt was Alex's blood. The judge also indicated there was no evidence showing that the t-shirt had been kept in a secure place since the date of the alleged incident, as it had not been provided to the police. Tracy's evidence was that she had left the t-shirt in the bedroom and when Alex could not attend Court, she decided to bring it along to prove what Jim had done.

Cross-Examination

On Jack's cross-examination of Tracy, she indicated that she had not seen Jim hit Alex. She indicated, however, that she knew he hit Alex because after Jim opened the bedroom door, Alex screamed and came out of the bedroom with a bloody nose. She said she was present when Jim made the death threats. She acknowledged that she did not know what affect the threats had on Alex and that Alex and Jim often used vulgar language when they were together.

Alex did not attend Court

Based on Jack's recommendation, Jim did not provide evidence.

Torcia State lawyer's submission

Alex did not testify but Tracy's evidence supports that Jim was uttering death threats to Alex and that Jim assaulted Alex who Tracy testified came out of his room with a bloody nose. Based on Tracy's evidence, Jim wanted money that Alex owed him for a car and when Alex did not have the money, Jim assaulted him and made death threats to him.

Jack's Submission to the Court:

Jack submitted that there was insufficient evidence to support a conviction on either charge. The key witness, Alex, did not attend court to provide evidence. Jack submitted that Tracy's evidence was not sufficient to support a conviction for either charge and that there was no direct evidence that Jim hit Alex.

Jack further submitted there was not sufficient evidence as to the effect Jim's words had on Alex given Tracy's acknowledgement Jim and Alex often used vulgar language with one another. Jack submitted that the State had not provided evidence to prove either charge beyond a reasonable doubt.

The Trial Court Decision:

Based on the evidence presented, the Trial Judge found there was not sufficient evidence to support a conviction for either charge. The judge stated that the law requires that the State prove the offences brought to Court beyond a reasonable doubt and that had not been done in the present case. The Trial Judge acquitted Jim on both charges.

Note to the Reader: The truth was not presented to the Court. Jack was not told the true story. The State did not know the true story. Tracy and Jim knew the true story but did not tell the truth. Alex did not come to Court because he did not want to tell the true story.

The True Story

Alex did not owe Jim money for a car but for drugs that Jim sold him. Jim was the local drug dealer who supplied marijuana and cocaine to people in the neighbourhood. Jim wanted the money Alex owed him for cocaine Jim had supplied to Alex. Jim went to the trailer to obtain his money. When Alex didn't have his money, he decided to teach Alex a lesson. There was no baseball bat. The bloodstained t-shirt was Alex's t-shirt from the incident and had been kept by Tracy but had not been provided to the police. Tracy did not want Alex to know she would be attending court to testify against Jim.

The reason Tracy gave evidence in Court was because she was angry with Jim for providing drugs to Alex. She wanted Jim to be sent to jail so he would stop supplying Alex with cocaine and marijuana. Alex had become addicted to cocaine and Tracy wanted to stop him from using the drug. She thought if her brother was in jail it would cut off Alex's drug supply and allow Alex to stop using drugs.

Alex did not attend Court was that he did not want to testify against Jim who continued to supply him with drugs.

The Judgement Game

1) Based on the material in this vignette, do you believe the judge made the right decision to acquit Jim?

Yes [ ] No [ ]

2) Based on your information as the omnipotent decision maker, would you have convicted Jim of assault?

Yes [ ] No [ ]

3) If you had convicted Jim, what sentence would you impose?

Absolute Discharge[8] ____

---

8 In Torcia, an absolute discharge means the offender will go free with only a written warning from the Court.

Conditional Discharge [9]____
If the discharge were conditional, what conditions would you impose? _____

_____

Fine ___
Probation with terms that Jim attends counselling for violence ___
Probation with terms that Jim attends drug-counselling ___
Jail ___
I want to impose my own sentence. It is:

_____

_____

_____

4) Based on your information as the omnipotent decision maker, would you have convicted Jim of uttering a death threat?
Yes ☐ No ☐

5) If you had convicted Jim of uttering a death threat, what sentence would you have imposed?
Absolute Discharge ___
Conditional Discharge ____
If the discharge were conditional, what conditions would you impose? _____

_____

Fine ___
Probation with terms that Jim attends counselling for violence ___
Probation with terms that Jim attends drug-counselling ___
Jail ___

---

9 A conditional discharge means the offender will go free on the conditions that you, the decision maker, set.

I want to impose my own sentence. It is:

_____

_____
_____

_____

Self-Assessment

You have the opportunity to provide a self-assessment after reading the vignettes in "The Omnipotent decision maker."

Indicate how many points* you give yourself for:

1) Recognition of issues raised in the chapter. ____

2) Suggestions and comments you made. ____

3) Your role as a decision maker. ____

TOTAL: ____

*You can give yourself 0 (lowest) to 5 (highest) points.
This is a game. Remember there are no right or wrong answers.

CHAPTER 5:
BOYS AND GIRLS BEHIND BARS

• • •

JOHNNY´S STORY – NATIONAL NEWS REPORT

At six o'clock, the prison night staff took over and the ordeal of inmate "Johnny" began. Several hours later, the alarm was sounded and Johnny was found dead in his cell. He had been tortured and killed by fellow inmates. The story was gruesome; an orgy of drugs, sex and the gang rape of Johnny by other inmates that ended with his involuntary hanging.

How many other murders and prison suicides will it take the public to recognise that the penitentiary system of Torcia does not work well for Torcian society or those it incarcerates? Is the public blinded by its wish to put Johnny and other inmates in a separate society, hoping they will be forgotten?

Who was Johnny? Was he not someone's child? Was he not someone's brother? Would Johnny have met a similar fate if he hadn't been in prison?

Statement of Prison Director
"Our prison did its best with limited resources and too many prisoners."

The prison director made no apologies and did not ask for an inquest into how this incident happened.

The Judgement Game
Should we listen to Johnny's story?

_____

_____

_____

What should we do about it?

_____

_____

_____

<u>MOVING OUT</u>

Prison is a different world, a world that defines its inhabitants by the risk they pose not only to society but also to others in the prison. Victor had become part of this world.

Victor had become a security risk in his home prison. He was suspected of being the leader of a group at the prison that was bringing drugs into the prison. He had been convicted of attempted murder for assaulting another inmate who had not paid for a quantity of drugs that Victor had provided the inmate. He had been convicted of assault on two previous occasions when Victor had not been paid for drugs. As a result, Victor was being transferred to a more secure facility.

He received notice that he was being transferred to a prison several thousand miles away from his home prison and his home community.

Victor's new home will be a tiny room at one of the high-security centres in Torcia. His room will be a two-and-a-half by three-metre steel cell where he cannot injure himself or others. The cell is supplied with a steel toilet, a small cot, and a desk. His food will arrive at specified hours and will be pushed through a small window that can only be opened from the outside. He will be allowed one hour of exercise each day. He will be able to read books and listen to music and the news on a small television/radio in his cell.

The Judgement Game
1) Did the prison system do the right thing in transferring Victor far away from his home prison?

_____

_____

_____

2) Did the prison system do the right thing by transferring Victor far away from his
home community?

_____

_____

_____

3) What are your suggestions for dealing with the threat Victor posed within his home prison?

_____

_____

_____

A GAME OF MOUSETRAP

George was a lawyer who handled cases for prison inmates. George received a call from an inmate at the prison indicating the inmate wanted to schedule an appointment with George. The inmate said he wanted to bring charges against a guard at the prison who has assaulted him and other inmates. He said there was a photo

George needed to see and that he would tell George the whole story when George came to the prison.

When George attended the prison to meet the inmate, the prison officer on duty suggested that George take extra precaution to the lawyer's interview room and showed George a panic button necklace which he suggested George wear. The officer indicated it would be wise to take the necklace in the event that the inmate decided to take George hostage. George could not understand this because George had been meeting inmates for several years without taking any special protection. What had changed?

The officer went on to say: "The prison service needs to be able to show what can happen when a lawyer takes the risk of meeting with these dangerous offenders. You have been meeting with several offenders that are unpredictable and dangerous. I am suggesting that you should take some extra protection with you when you go to the interview room. I'm telling you this for your own safety."

George focused on the guard's words: "<u>The prison service needs to be able to show what can happen</u> when a lawyer takes the risk of meeting with these dangerous offenders." Was the officer warning George that something was going to happen?

George knew that lawyers' conversations with inmates were intercepted by the prison service. The service would have heard there were allegations that a guard had assaulted inmates including the inmate who called George. The service would also have heard there was photo evidence of the assault that was to be provided to George.

George's mind envisaged the news report: "Guard at High Maximum Prison shoots inmate and lawyer in attempt to stop hostage taking"!

What do we know about the mousetrap?
We know mice live in the prisons and generally scamper about freely. We know that from time to time, should a mouse scamper about too much or become too noisy, the prison service will set its

mousetrap to catch the mouse. What we do not know is whether the mousetrap is also set to catch lawyers.

Should George take the risk of interviewing the inmate without protection?

Yes___ No___

Why or Why Not?

_____

_____

_____

Was the panic necklace a protection or a set- up?

Protection ___

Set-Up ___

The Judgement Game

1)   Was the prison setting the mousetrap for the inmate who called George?

Yes [ ] No [ ]

2)   Was the prison setting the mousetrap for George?

Yes [ ] No [ ]

3) Would there be regret by the prison should an inmate be caught in the mousetrap?

Yes [ ] No [ ]

4) Would there be regret by the prison should a lawyer be caught in the mousetrap?

Yes [ ] No [ ]

5) Would there be regret by the public should an inmate be caught in the mousetrap?

Yes [ ] No [ ]

6) Would there be regret by the public should a lawyer be caught in the mousetrap?

Yes ☐ No ☐

OBEYING THE RULES

Bryan was an attractive boy of seventeen when he entered prison. He used his intelligence to survive in prison, but he knew it was his body that had more value in the prison setting. Men at the prison who wanted sexual relationships coveted him. After being raped by two men, high in the inmate hierarchy, Bryan learnt he needed to gain protection from these types of activities by becoming another inmate's "boy", more bluntly, another inmate's "prison wife." To be somebody's "boy" gave that man ownership rights that were respected by other inmates in the prison.

Bryan decided to look for an inmate who would be able to provide him protection, someone with a high profile in the prison because of the length of time the man was serving, and someone with status because of the type of crimes he had committed.

Bryan learnt Simon had been incarcerated for drug offences and was one of the key players in the drug trade at the prison. Bryan found him to be a decent fellow and offered to become Simon's "boy". Simon was not an attractive man; acne having left his face scarred. He was also slightly overweight. Bryan, on the other hand, was slim and kept himself fit by working out regularly in the prison gym.

Simon was pleased when he leant that Bryan was willing to be his "boy". Simon didn't ask Bryan for much except regular sexual relations, no "kinky stuff." Simon also asked for Bryan's fidelity.

Simon wanted Bryan to share time with him using the drugs Simon was able to bring into the prison. Simon asked Bryan to steal fruit and vegetables from the kitchen, where Bryan was working, so they could make "hooch," an alcoholic prison drink they both enjoyed.

Their lives went along without hassle until the structure of the prison population changed. Bryan and Simon were both maximum-security prisoners. The prison was re-classified from maximum security to become a facility that housed both maximum-security and medium-security inmates. This became a problem for Simon and Bryan because the new medium-security prisoners were unfamiliar with the prison code and rules of inmate hierarchy followed by the lifers and maximum-security inmates.

The problem became apparent when a new medium-security inmate, Mel, decided to hit on Bryan. He was discreetly told by other prisoners to back off because Bryan was Simon's "boy". Mel didn't listen and continued his pursuit. The situation was even more of a problem because Bryan and Mel both worked in the kitchen where they were often in close contact.

News of Mel's pursuit of Bryan travelled quickly. When Simon heard the news, he took steps to contact other inmates who worked in the kitchen to find out if Bryan was playing around on him. Mel was a good-looking man and closer in age to Bryan than Simon. Word came back to Simon that Mel was the pursuer and would not leave Bryan alone. As a result, Simon decided Mel needed to be given a warning.

After finishing work one afternoon, Mel returned to his unit and opened his cell door to find a plate of raw calf testicles on his bed. Beside the meat was a note: "Best you get out of the kitchen." Mel paid no attention to the message and continued his work in the kitchen and his pursuit of Bryan.

The next message from Simon was not as subtle. When Mel was making his way to the gym, he was accosted by a group of inmates and escorted to a corner of the courtyard. There, Mel was given some private "yoga" lessons that left him limping for a week. He was told by his "yoga" instructors that unless he wanted to sing soprano, he had better get out of the kitchen and leave Bryan alone. The next day Mel applied for and was granted a transfer from his work in the kitchen to new work in the metal shop.

Guards and prison authorities often turn a blind eye to sexual activities taking place in prisons in order to keep peace within the prison walls. The prison is, however, a community and there are rules in that community. Mel had to learn the importance of obeying the rules.

The Judgement Game

1) Is the prison code followed by the lifers and maximum-security inmates described in this vignette justified?

_____

_____

_____

Why or why not?

_____

_____

_____

2) Should the prison have brought internal disciplinary charges against Simon for organizing the assault on Mel?

Yes ☐ No ☐

Why or why not?

_____

_____

_____

3) Should the prison have brought internal disciplinary charges against the "yoga" instructors for assaulting Mel?

Yes ☐ No ☐

Why or why not?

_____

_____

_____

4) Should Mel have brought criminal charges against the yoga¨ instructors for assaulting Mel?

Yes [   ] No [   ]

Why or why not?

_____

_____

_____

PRISON ATTRACTION

I was six years old the first time I saw the prison. It was a group of buildings off the main highway. The buildings, which were set back from the road, intrigued me and had an impressive entrance flanked by a row of large oak trees. A large, round, green water tower allowed the buildings to be seen from a distance.

When we were driving past the buildings, I asked my father what the buildings were. He said it was a prison, a place for "bad boys." I asked dad if we could stop to visit the "bad boys." He said we could not stop because it was not the kind of place for good little boys like me. I was upset because I did not want to be classified as a good boy. I wanted to have fun. I wanted to find out who the "bad boys" were and why they lived there.

I looked at the prison every time we travelled down that highway. It was a fascinating and mysterious place for me to think about. I was frightened of the bad boys without knowing anything about them. I kept thinking about the bad things that they must have done to be sent to prison. I envisaged the robberies, thefts and assaults the "bad boys" must have committed. My mind was intrigued and I spent my journeys creating mysteries about the crimes they had committed.

When we passed the prison I looked for signs of life and for the "bad boys." The prison remained silent and there was no sign of the "bad boys". I was sure they were there because dad said they were there.

It was not until I was an adult that I went back to the prison. In fact, I was not given a choice about which prison I would be sent to. The prison was a medium-security institution that housed offenders in protective custody, men who had committed unspeakable crimes. We are considered "bad boys" by the prison system, by fellow inmates and by society.

You probably want to know what I did to become one of the "bad boys". I am a middle-aged man, forty-five years old and starting to go bald. I wear glasses and have a small paunch from drinking too much beer. I'm a bank manager and work for a well-known national bank in Jervis.

I was convicted of sexually assaulting a boy in the park I often go to. I was surprised when I was told the boy was only fourteen years old because he had all of the tools of a man.

Across the street from the park, I knew I could have had female flesh, little girls in jolly mini-skirts. I had tried that before, but it is not what I crave. That is not what satisfies my desires. I wanted those sculptured busts and bottoms like the statues of the young soldiers in the park.

My love child was wearing army fatigues and army boots. For me that was an invitation for an evening of high adventure. He didn't ask for money, but I had it ready, and he didn't refuse to take it.

I didn't know I had an audience that evening. The police must have waited for me to stroll around the park taking pictures of the statues and trees before I saw the young man and made my approach. I saw a film of me taking pictures, admiring the statues of the soldiers and I saw the details of my conquest. With that evidence, it was hard to say it wasn't me. That is why I am now one of the "bad boys".

My family didn't know about my desire to have sex with young boys. The psychiatrist told the Court I'm a paedophile. That word makes me shudder. I do not think I am a paedophile because I like men and women too, although I don't like them as much.

I should have taken the young fellow to a hotel, but my desire to have him was too great. The police found us together beside the statue of a young soldier, where my love child was satisfying me. The police did not look the other way. The charges against me were thorough: indecent exposure, engaging in sexual activities with a minor, abetting prostitution.

The police called my wife. She came to the police station. I think she was shocked to find me there, no matter what I had done. She was quiet and reserved, but I could feel her cold eyes judging me as unworthy to be her husband. I didn't know what to say to her. All I could think of to say was, "sorry, dear."

My wife will tell our children I'm working out of town. At some point they will need to know what I did but not now; they are too young.

I took a leave of absence from my job after I was arrested. I know criminal convictions for these charges will mean I can't return to my profession as a banker or my position as a bank manager. Strict rules in my profession do not allow members to have criminal records. That problem, however, was far from my mind. It was my safety that I was concerned about.

The most important thing for me was that I have protective custody. I didn't want to be killed by other inmates should they find out I am not a drug dealer caught selling drugs to a boy in the park. That is what I told them at the prison placement centre where I was sent before sentencing.

I have now been sentenced. The Court awarded a global sentence of ten years for my offences.

Prison placement has been arranged. I will go back to the prison along the highway that I had first seen when I was a child. I've now been formally classified by the medical professionals as a paedophile. I can now be welcomed to the prison for "bad boys". I will be placed with my own.

I've now found out who the "bad boys" are and what they do. It is now my home.

The Judgement Game

1) Was the ten-year global sentence given to the offender in Prison Attraction the only punishment the offender received?

Yes ☐ No ☐

If not, what other punishment did he receive?

_____

_____

_____

2) What sentence would you recommend for the offender?

_____

_____

_____

3) Was the offender's concern that he receives protective custody justified?

Yes ☐ No ☐

TORCIA´S PRISONS

1) From the news reports, what problems need to be addressed in Torcia's prisons?

*See also Mary's Story in Chapter 6

_____

_____

_____

2) What can be done to deal with these problems?

_____

_____

_____

3) Will there always be a role for prisons in Torcia?

Yes ☐   No ☐

If so, why?

_____

_____

_____

Self-Assessment

You have the opportunity to provide a self-assessment after reading the vignettes in ¨Boys and Girls Behind Bars¨.

   Indicate how many points* you give yourself for:

   1) Recognition of issues raised in the chapter.   ____

   2) Suggestions and comments you made.   ____

   3) Your role as a decision maker.   ____

   TOTAL: ____

*You can give yourself 0 (lowest) to 5 (highest) points.

This is a game. Remember there are no right or wrong answers.

CHAPTER 6:
DRUG OFFENCES - WAR
AGAINST DRUGS

•   •   •

MARY´S STORY

Mary is serving a seven-year sentence at Deerfoot Prison for organizing a prostitution ring in Jervis. At Deerfoot Prison Mary became involved in a prison drug war and was charged with assaulting another inmate, Betty, a key player in bringing drugs into Deerfoot Prison.

Mary comes from a Mexian family living on a housing estate in Jervis. Mary has seven brothers and sisters. Three of her brothers are in jail for thefts and robberies. Two brothers and their families live and work in the city of Jervis and her two sisters are married and live in different cities. She has stayed in touch with her parents on the housing estate but only sporadically with her siblings.

Mary was sexually assaulted as a child by her uncle and by her eldest brother. She never told her parents about these incidents.

Mary left school at the age of thirteen and started looking for work. She was given the name of a beauty school in Jervis that turned out to be a front for prostitution services. She provided services to the beauty school's clients for five years and took the money home to help support her family. Her parents did not ask where she was working or what type of work she was doing. Mary believes they had known what kind of work she was doing but didn't want to talk about it. Like other young women with Mexian backgrounds, Mary found the easiest way to make money was as a prostitute.

After becoming a prostitute, Mary used drugs in an attempt to escape and detach her mind from her body. Unfortunately, her drug use became addictive and she found it necessary to feed her habit on a regular basis.

Mary decided to leave her association with the beauty school and branch out on her own. She organized a prostitution ring in her neighbourhood in Jervis, which she operated for several years before she was arrested and convicted of the charge that brought her to Deerfoot Prison.

At Deerfoot Prison, Mary's use of drugs started out as personal but because of her profile as a Mexian inmate and the competition between different groups in the prison to control the drug trade, Mary became involved in trying to win control of the trade for the Mexian inmates.

During an incident at Deerfoot, Betty was stabbed in the chest with a knife. The wound was superficial. The prison contacted the police who, following investigation, charged Mary with assault with a deadly weapon.

After discussions with her lawyer, Mary entered a guilty plea to assault with a deadly weapon.

The only question for you, the sentencing authority, is the length of sentence to be imposed on Mary for assault with a deadly weapon. The maximum penalty for the offence is twenty years imprisonment. There is no mandatory minimum sentence.

Torcia State lawyer's Submission

My submission is that you should impose a sentence of five years given the injuries sustained by Betty. Mary violently assaulted Betty with a deadly weapon and intended to inflict grievous bodily harm on her. Her punishment must reflect that.

Mary's Lawyer's Submission

It is submitted that this offence of assault was an unfortunate result of prison life and a drug war that Mary became involved in. Two groups at Deerfoot prison wanted control of the drug trade. Mary, a representative of the Mexian group, was elected to confront Betty the leader of the competing group. Mary had little choice but to accept her role as representative of the Mexian group to which she was aligned because of race and culture.

Mary has little education, having stopped attending school at the age of thirteen. She has, however, considerable talent in painting. Mary paints pictures of traditional symbols and ancient legends of the Mexian people. Prior to her incarceration, Mary had contacted art galleries in Jervis and the neighbouring city of Reda. She had been asked to submit her work to two galleries but because of her arrest and incarceration was not able to pursue those opportunities.

My submission is that the sentence you impose should recognise there might be an opportunity for Mary to leave the prison world and make her name in the world of art. Unlike many, Mary has a skill that can take her away from the world of crime that she has become part of. Mary acknowledges that she must obtain assistance to deal with her drug problem. She advises she is prepared to take drug counselling.

It is submitted that a fit sentence in this case would be two years with a recommendation from the Court that Mary attend the drug-counselling programme offered at the prison during that two-year period. It is submitted this sentence recognises the severity of the offence but also recognises the circumstances of the offender.

The Judgement Game

1) What sentence do you impose on Mary?

a) The sentence recommended by the Torcia State lawyer: five years incarceration.

Yes ☐

No ☐

b) The sentence recommended by Mary's counsel, two years incarceration, with a recommendation Mary attends drug counselling during that two-year period.

Yes ☐

No ☐

c) Do you believe incarceration is the best way to respond to this offence?

Yes ☐

No ☐

d) I want to impose my own sentence. It is:

_____

_____

_____

e) What other possible sentences would you suggest?

_____

_____

_____

PETRA AND WOLF

Wolf, a man Petra met at a bar in Reda where she was working, contacted her to say he was looking for a reliable person to work with him as a sales representative at his business, Celebrity Shoes, a company that sold designer shoes. He told Petra he was able to purchase and bring the latest models of shoes from the neighbouring country of Geliva under a trade agreement between the two countries. Wolf told Petra that Celebrity Shoes could purchase the shoes for a good price in Gcliva and bring them to Reda where they would be sold. Wolf told her the job would involve travelling to the city of San Miguel in Geliva to deliver money, pick up the newest styles of shoes and bring the shoes back to him at Celebrity Shoes.

Petra is a single parent. She had a baby when she was seventeen years-old. Her boyfriend had abandoned her after the baby was born and never provided any financial support for Petra or her child. Petra, now twenty-one years old, moved from one bar job to another in order to make a living.

Wolf told Petra that it was important for his business that he keeps pace with the latest shoe designs from Geliva. He said Petra would be a good sales representative for Celebrity Shoes because of her youth and her ability to deal with people. Petra thought this sounded like a good opportunity although she was surprised by Wolf's offer given she had only met Wolf on two occasions when he came to the bar where she was working.

Petra took the job and made several trips to San Miguel. Wolf paid for Petra to fly to San Miguel and deliver the purchase money to Wolf's contacts so that she could pick up the newest designs of shoes and bring them back to Wolf at Celebrity Shoes. Wolf gave her money to pay for hotels and to cover her expenses. He also paid her a good salary.

All was going well for Petra until Wolf decided to change Petra's instructions. Although Petra would continue to go to San Miguel to pick up shoes, Wolf told her these shoes would be packed with packages of heroin. Wolf told Petra that her salary would be doubled if she agreed to bring the shoes back to Reda as instructed. He said the additional money would benefit Petra and her daughter, Joli. Petra had been required to hire a caregiver for Joli when she made trips to San Miguel and knew the extra money would come in handy.

Petra didn't want to lose her job because her work for Celebrity Shoes was the first time she had been able to support herself and Joli comfortably. Petra decided she would follow Wolf's instructions, even though she knew there was a risk of her being caught.

Wolf told her that not all of the shoes she would be bringing back would contain heroin because he had to ensure that Celebrity Shoes looked like a legitimate company. Wolf also told her that the Gelivian shoe designers would be inserting secret compartments in the soles of some of the shoes where heroin could be packed.

Petra agreed to continue the shoe deliveries not only because of the income it gave her but also because the job allowed her to spend more time with her daughter Joli. She knew that she would not have that opportunity if she had a regular, nine-to-five job. When she was at home, she spent evenings with her daughter playing games, singing songs and reading fairy tales. Joli had just turned four and her favourite fairy tale was Little Red Riding Hood. Joli paid particular attention to the wolf in the Little Red Riding Hood story. She asked Petra if Petra's boss, Wolf, was a bad wolf like the one in the story or if he was a good wolf. Petra told Joli that her boss was a good wolf because he gave mommy a good job so she could bring presents home for Joli.

The shoe deliveries continued without problem for two years. Petra recalls that Joli was turning six years old the day that a major drug delivery from San Miguel had been scheduled. Petra had been instructed by Wolf to pick up a new design of party shoes called "the Rudolf shoes" which the Geliva crafts people had made for the Christmas market. Wolf told her the heroin to be brought to Reda with that delivery would be packed in a secret compartment of the Rudolf shoes.

Unfortunately, things did not go well when Petra arrived at airport customs. A customs officer asked to inspect her carry on luggage and her shoes. Petra placed her carry on luggage, which included the birthday gift she had bought for Joli, a Red Riding Hood doll, and the Rudolf shoes, on the counter.

Fortunately, for Petra, the crafts people in Geliva had designed the Rudolf shoes so well that the heroin packed in the secret compartment was not found by the officer or the drug dog inspecting the shoes. The drug dog reacted, however, to the Red Riding Hood Doll in the hand luggage. When the dog sniffed the luggage, the dog tried to eat the Red Riding Hood doll. The dog's reaction caused the customs officer to rip the doll open to see if it contained drugs. He found no drugs, only regular stuffing.

The customs officer checked Petra's passport to verify her name and asked her to provide her current address. He kept what remained of the doll but let Petra go through customs. Petra knew that even though she was able to proceed through customs and return to Reda, it was likely that the problem would resurface once she was back in Reda. She knew she would need to tell Wolf what happened when she delivered the Rudolf shoes and drugs to him the next day.

Because of the time taken examining her luggage and the shoes, Petra missed the flight she had been scheduled to take and had to take a later flight. The delay resulted in her not arriving home in time for Joli´s birthday party. As well, she had no gift for Joli because the customs authorities had confiscated the Red Riding Hood doll. Thus, she arrived home late and empty-handed.

When Petra went to Celebrity Shoes the following day, she told Wolf what had happened. Wolf's response was that because of the way the drug dog had reacted, Petra wouldn't be required to make further trips to San Miguel. Wolf said she was, because of the incident at customs, suspected of having been in possession of drugs and he did not want to take further risk of having her bring drugs to Reda. He told her he would pay her for the work she had done but she was to have no further contact with him or Celebrity Shoes.

Petra was shocked by what had happened and how quickly her life had changed. She was, again, without work.

Three weeks later two police officers arrived at the door of Petra's house. Fortunately, Joli had left for play-school. After asking Petra to acknowledge she was Petra Bevan, the police arrested her for several counts of importing heroin. She was taken to the police station, where she was asked more questions about her job as sales representative for Wolf and Celebrity Shoes. She decided it would not be wise to give the police more information and told the officers that she did not want to say anything. She did not want Wolf to think she was a "rat" who provided information to the police.

After being charged, Petra contacted a lawyer at Torcia's Legal Assistance programme. After two meetings with the lawyer, Petra was given astounding news. The lawyer told her that he had learnt that Wolf was an undercover agent for the drug investigation unit in Reda. The lawyer explained to Petra that police investigations of drug offences in Torcia commonly involved the use of undercover officers.

Torcia had passed legislation to make otherwise unlawful conduct by the police (such as entrapment) legal, provided it was authorised as part of a controlled operation. The lawyer said police investigations into drug offences commonly involved the use of undercover officers who either offered a degree of encouragement to people to commit an offence, or to participate in criminal activity, or both. He indicated he learnt that the police investigation Wolf was involved in was a controlled operation intended to deter Torcian citizens from importing drugs from Geliva. Apparently, Geliva had become a major avenue for bringing drugs into Reda and other cities in Torcia.

The lawyer told her that there was no substantive defence of entrapment in Torcian law for drug offences, so she would not be able to argue entrapment as a defence to the charge of importing heroin. The lawyer recommended that Petra enter a guilty plea and hope for a light sentence.

Petra found out the drug investigation unit had photos of her coming through customs on ten separate occasions and Wolf had taken pictures of her handing shoes containing heroin over to him on each occasion, including the last trip when she handed him the Rudolf shoes containing the drugs. Each photo showed the shoes, the secret compartments where the drugs had been packed in the shoes, as well as the heroin that had been provided to Wolf on each occasion.

Petra entered guilty pleas to the ten offences of importing heroin. The Court has not yet provided sentence as it is awaiting sentencing submissions from the Torcia State lawyer and Petra's lawyer.

You are to provide your comments and make the following decisions about this vignette:

1) Was Wolf a good wolf or a bad wolf?
Good ___ Bad ___

2) Do you believe that the drug laws of Torcia set out in this vignette and the definition of entrapment in Annex B are justified?
Yes [ ] No [ ]

3) Are there any morals to be learnt from the story, Petra and Wolf?

_____

_____

_____

THE COST OF BUSINESS

The anti-crime brigade of Jervis arrested a twenty-two-year-old man suspected of trafficking in drugs in the Bowna area. The young man was stopped by chance when the police were responding to a call regarding an alleged assault. The police found six hundred and seventy five grams of cannabis resin, electronic scales, and a significant amount of cash in the possession of the young man. The suspect acknowledged the drugs were his, but stated they were for his personal use.

The young man had been arrested three months ago for possession of three hundred grams of hashish. When he had attended Court on that occasion, he had entered a guilty plea and had been placed on probation for six months with conditions that he keep the peace and be of good behaviour and take drug counselling.

The young man decided to plead guilty to the breach of probation for failing to keep the peace and be of good behaviour. Probation service records show he is enrolled in a drug-counselling course and has attended all meetings with his probation officer.

He entered a not guilty plea to the new charge of trafficking in a narcotic for the six-hundred and seventy-five grams of cannabis resin found by the police. The Court set a trial date for that matter and the Court will deal with the matter on a subsequent occasion. You should recognize that the young man is innocent until proven guilty of the charge of trafficking.

You are asked to make a recommendation for the sentencing principles to be applied in dealing with this young man.

The young man has no legal representation. He has advised you that he wants to handle this matter on this own. He submits that the hashish for which he was arrested three months ago was for his personal use. He indicates he had no previous criminal record for drug offences prior to the offence three months ago.

The Torcia State lawyer advises that while the young man had no criminal record for drug offences, he did have a criminal record for another offence, the offence of theft under $1000 that had occurred two years ago. At that time, he had been given a conditional discharge specifying that he repay the victim and also that he provide fifty hours community service. Court records show that this sentence was successfully completed.

You are asked to make a recommendation as to the objectives you want to achieve in responding to the current activities of this young man.

The Judgement Game
1) Your recommendation:
What sentencing objectives[10] do you want to promote?
General Deterrence (for others)
Individual Deterrence (for the offender) ___
Rehabilitation ____
Retribution ___
Restorative Justice ____
What are your suggestions about how to deal with this offender?

_____
_____
_____

What effect does the fact he has been charged with trafficking although he has not yet convicted have on your recommendation?

_____
_____
_____

In your opinion, was it wise that he decided to enter a guilty plea to the breach of probation charge without retaining legal counsel?
Yes ☐ No ☐

Why or Why not?

_____
_____
_____

10 See Annex A

111

Are you in favour of him completing the drug-counselling course that he started as part of his probation order?

Yes ☐ No ☐

Why or Why Not?

_____

_____

_____

PLAYING WITH POSSESSION[11]

In this series of reports, you will be given the opportunity to work with the legal provisions and drug laws of possession set out in Torcia´s drug laws. You will need to refer to the legislation provided in the Annex B. You will interpret the words set out. The cases appear to be the same or almost the same; however, on close review you will see the cases are different.

Case No. 1 – GOOD FRIEND (GF)

The key issue here was whether GF, the co-tenant of a house who was charged with possession of marijuana for trafficking and production of a controlled substance, had sufficient knowledge and control.

GF was a co-tenant of a house where the police found two hundred and fifty marijuana plants growing in a garage located next to the house. They also found twenty plants in a bedroom of the house and two bags of marijuana in a second bedroom of the house along with a set of scales and a book about growing marijuana.

In this case, GF did not admit direct connection to the grow operation in any way (such as watering or tending the plants).

---

11 See Definitions in Annex B

GF was acquitted by the Trial Court because:

1. The grow operation was conducted in a separate garage on the property, and there was no evidence to show GF had a key that unlocked the garage.
2. There was no evidence to show that GF had access to the bedroom, where more marijuana plants were found, or to a second bedroom, where two bags of marijuana, a set of scales and a book about growing marijuana had been found.

The Court found that the State had not proved either knowledge or control beyond a reasonable doubt so GF was acquitted.

The Court was not satisfied beyond a reasonable doubt of GF's guilt. It held that knowledge is not the only rational inference one can draw from there being marijuana, scales and a book about marijuana in the house where GF was a co-tenant. It was pointed out that there is no evidence that GF was able to gain access to the grow operation with a key or that GF played a role in the grow operation.

The Court went on to say that, the question of control is even more problematic. There was no evidence GF had control over the grow operation. Even in GF knew of the presence of the marijuana, control had to be proved beyond a reasonable doubt and that had not been done.

The Judgement Game

1) Was this acquittal justified?

Yes ☐ No ☐

2) If you had convicted GF, what sentence would you impose?

Absolute Discharge[12] ____

----

12 An absolute discharge means the offender will go free with only a written warning from the Court.

Conditional Discharge[13] ____

If the discharge were conditional, what conditions would you impose?

_____

_____

_____

Fine ____

Probation on terms that GF take drug-counselling ____

Jail ____

I want to impose my own sentence. It is:

_____

_____

_____

Case No. 2 – Unfortunate Friend (UF)

UF was living in a house that had 191 marijuana plants growing in the basement. UF was charged with possession of marijuana for the purposes of trafficking. The Court looked for elements of knowledge and control.

The Court said the following facts satisfied the requirement for control:

- UF had access to the residence;
- There was no lock on the basement door;
- UF was living in the house and UF´s furnishings were in the house;
- Documents and a vehicle found at the residence belonged to UF;
- The marijuana plants in the basement had to be hand watered every day or every other day.

---

13 A conditional discharge means the offender will be released on the conditions that you, the decision-maker, set.

The Court said the following facts indicated sufficient knowledge:
1. Strong smell of marijuana throughout the house;
2. Marijuana poster in the kitchen UF was using;
3. Marijuana bud found in the UF´s bathroom.

UF was convicted of possession of marijuana for trafficking and was sentenced to spend eighteen months in jail.

The Judgement Game
If you do not agree with the Trial Court decision for UF, what sentence would you impose?
Absolute Discharge [14]____
Conditional Discharge[15]
If the discharge were conditional, what conditions would you impose?

_____

_____

_____

Fine ____
Probation on terms that UF take drug-counselling ____
Jail ____
I want to recommend my own sentence. It is:

_____

_____

_____

Your Response to the War against drugs:
1) How should Torcia's justice system respond to drug offences?
   • With training courses for offenders?
   Yes [ ] No [ ]

14 An absolute discharge means the offender will go free with only a written warning from the Court.
15 A conditional discharge means the offender will be released on the conditions that you, the decision maker, set.

- With incarceration of offenders?

Yes [ ] No [ ]

- With fines?

Yes [ ] No [ ]

- With educational information provided to Torcia's citizens.

Yes [ ] No [ ]

2) Do you believe drug offences are business, crime, or both business and crime?

_____

_____

_____

3) What does this vignette show about the responses of Torcia's criminal justice system to drug offences?

_____

_____

_____

4) Provide your Comments about the definitions of possession, knowledge and control that you worked with in this vignette:

_____

_____

_____

Self-Assessment

You have the opportunity to provide a self-assessment after reading the vignettes in "Drug Offences: War Against Drugs."

    Indicate how many points* you give yourself for:

1) Recognition of issues raised in the chapter. ___
2) Suggestions and comments you made. ___
3) Your role as a decision maker. ___

TOTAL: ___

*You can give yourself 0 (lowest) to 5 (highest) points.
This is a game. Remember there are no right or wrong answers.

CHAPTER 7:
HOME INVASION AND BREACH OF TRUST

• • •

HOME SWEET HOME

My name is Ben Husse. I am sixty-five years old and recently retired. Before I retired, I owned my own business, Hussencraft Inc. and spent many years working as a carpenter producing handcrafted furniture for people's homes. I learnt my craft from artisans in my country, Balicia, a country that prides itself in producing the finest furniture.

Prior to coming to Torcia, I completed three years of mandatory military service in Balicia. Civil strife in Balicia has been going on for decades and I was happy to move to Torcia, a young country with the reputation of being united and calm.

Now that I am retired, I spend a great deal of time at home. I can sleep as long as I want because I have no need to get out of bed early. I am alone at the house. My wife and I are separated. She lives at our daughter's house in a granny flat they built for her and she looks after our daughter's three children. I keep in touch with my two granddaughters and grandson at Christmas and for their birthdays.

At about eleven o'clock one morning, I heard the doorbell ring. I had recently ordered a new television for which I was awaiting delivery. I believed the doorbell was announcing the arrival of my new television. I got up, slipped into the bottom half of my tracksuit, and ran downstairs. The doorbell rang again.

"Bloody hell, I'm coming, I'm coming," I called out.

I opened the door without looking through the peephole and was greeted by two figures with hoods. One of the men pointed a pistol in my face and said, "Gim´me your wallet."

My first reaction was one of anger. Instead of doing what he demanded, I struck out with my fist, knocking the gun from his hand. The gun flipped back and hit him in the face before falling to the floor. The other man just stood there. I was able to grab the gun before the men rushed toward me. I had no time to think and pulled the trigger. The bullet hit the man who had initially threatened me, and he fell to the floor. I was still holding the gun. The other man didn't move. He stood like a statue in front of me.

"Don't shoot," he whined.

I was in shock. I looked down to see if the man I shot was alive. He was lying on the floor; there was no sound, no movement. He was not breathing and, clearly, he was dead. There was no blood, nothing. His eyes were open, and he looked like someone that had fallen and was unable to get up.

I looked at the other man and said, "Come with me. I have to phone the police."

He followed me to the kitchen. My legs and hands were shaking, but I kept the gun pointed at the man walking beside me to ensure he did not try to overpower me.

I called the emergency police number. I asked for immediate assistance.

When the police arrived, I was still holding the gun and had it pointed at the man. One of the two police officers took the gun away from me and told me and the man to take seats in the kitchen. The man told the police I had threatened to kill him. I tried to explain to the police what had happened that morning but the officers would not listen to me.

I was shocked by what the police did. They placed both me and the other man in custody and took both of us to the police station. After being booked in at the station, I was placed in a cell and told I could call a lawyer. I told the police I did not want to talk to a lawyer, as I had done nothing wrong. I told them I had been defending myself.

After being in the cell for what seemed like an eternity, an officer came by to tell me that I would be charged with murder[16]. I could not believe what I was hearing. Shit, I was defending my property and myself. I shouldn't be charged with anything. What was I supposed to do, let the robbers kill me? I was defending myself. I didn't do anything wrong.

I will plead not guilty. This is bullshit. Surely, they can't send me to jail for this! I know Torcia law allows me to defend my property and myself. The Court will see I did not intend to kill that son of a bitch. I had no choice. I was defending myself.

I learnt that the police charged the other fellow with home invasion, a charge that carries a maximum penalty of ten years in jail. That bastard may get ten years or less, and I may get life.

The Judgement Game

1) Did Ben use reasonable force to defend himself?

Yes [ ] No [ ]

Why or Why Not?

_____

_____

_____

2) Should Ben be convicted of murder?

Yes [ ] No [ ]

Why or Why Not?

_____

_____

_____

16 See Definitions of Murder and Manslaughter and Self-Defence in the Annex B

3) Should Ben be convicted of manslaughter?

Yes ☐ No ☐

Why or Why Not?

_____

_____

_____

4) Should Ben be acquitted?

Yes ☐ No ☐

Why or Why Not?

_____

_____

_____

THIS IS NOT A FAIRY TALE

Fonsilla worked all her life to help her family. Her family had acquired a significant parcel of land near the city of Hortus in Torcia. It was an enchanting land full of trees and animals and was known by everyone in the area as Paradisimo. Fonsilla's parents left the property to her in their wills because they knew she would care for it. Her parents did not leave the property to Fonsilla's two sisters, Gladisa and Elsa because they knew Gladisa and Elsa did not want the Paradisimo property but only money. Fonsilla's parents left Gladisa and Elsa enough money to look after themselves during their lives, but no part of the Paradisimo property.

Two years after Fonsilla's parents had passed away, Fonsilla met Principe Carmo, known as PC. PC's family was not wealthy and PC had few prospects for obtaining work. He had grown up in a farming community in his country, Geliva. His parents were small land

122

owners who raised cattle and horses. He had always worked with horses and wanted to find work with private stables in Torcia.

Fonsilla met PC at a horse show where she was showing her horse. He was working as a stable hand cleaning stalls and providing general services to the owners of the horses being shown. As it happened, PC was cleaning the stall of Fonsilla's horse.

When Fonsilla saw PC, she was taken by how handsome he was and wanted to get to know him. She walked over to speak to him and found him to be charming and agreeable. She mentioned to PC that her horse needed new shoes because it had lost one of its shoes when she arrived at the horse show. PC indicated that he was willing to look for quality shoes for her horse.

PC was captivated by Fonsilla's beauty. He knew immediately he had found the woman of his dreams. He wanted to impress her by providing special shoes for her horse. After searching his farrier's catalogue for styles, he decided to put diamond studded shoes on Fonsilla's horse. He believed it was important to make a good and lasting impression on lovely Fonsilla.

When Fonsilla saw PC's work she was astounded by the elegance of the diamond studded shoes and how well the shoes had been fitted. Fonsilla was so impressed with his work she decided to give him a job looking after the stable at Paradisimo. This gave Fonsilla and PC the opportunity to spend time together. Their relationship turned quickly into one of romance. Fonsilla had never met such a gracious and loving man as PC and she was swept off her feet by his love and attention.

Within months PC asked Fonsilla to marry him. Fonsilla accepted PC's marriage proposal. She knew she had more money and property than PC, but that he did not want her money or property but to build a life with her at Paradisimo.

Following their marriage, PC and Fonsilla established their home at Paradisimo. They built a fairytale mansion and created a deer park on the property. They lived with nature and animals around them and were happy.

A year after their marriage, Fonsilla gave birth to a baby girl. She and PC decided to call the baby Carmella.

Paradisimo was close to the large city, Hortus. Hortus was expanding rapidly, and real estate agents approached Fonsilla and PC trying to purchase the Paradisimo lands. Realtors wanted to build housing estates and commercial centers on the property. Fonsilla and PC rejected all offers because they wanted Paradisimo to become a game reserve to protect the animals and the native land of Torcia. Fonsilla knew that her parents would have wanted their property to be protected and kept in a natural state for the enjoyment of Fonsilla and her family.

PC was not, however, able to keep Fonsilla´s aunts, Gladisa and Elsa away from Fonsilla and Paradisimo. Although Gladisa and Elsa had enough money to live comfortably, they were jealous of the love Fonsilla had found with PC as well as Fonsilla´s decision to have a baby. As they had no husbands or children, they sought to steal the affection of little Carmella from PC and Fonsilla. They bought expensive gifts for Carmella in an attempt to gain her favor at an early age.

PC warned Fonsilla about what her sisters were doing, but Fonsilla believed in the importance of family ties. She told PC she did not want to cut her sisters off from Carmella.

Neither she nor PC was aware that Gladisa and Elsa had made an agreement with Ramon, a young solicitor in Hortus, with the intention of regaining ownership of the Paradisimo property. Their plan was to have Ramon work with them to trick Carmella into doing what they wanted with Paradisimo. They knew that sweet innocent Carmella could be easily influenced.

Their plots started by having Ramon convince Fonsilla and PC to place the Paradisimo property in trust for Carmella. When Carmella would reach the age of eighteen, the trust would take effect and the Paradisimo property would become hers. That would give them time enough to work with Ramon to shape Carmella's ideas so that she would do what they and Ramon wanted her to do.

Following Gladisa and Elsa's instructions, Ramon met with PC and Fonsilla to speak to them about creating the trust of the Paradisimo property for Carmella, with a life interest in a small parcel of the property to be reserved for PC and Fonsilla. Ramon told them this would be beneficial for estate planning because it would lessen the tax burden to be paid by Carmella when Fonsilla and PC passed away. He also assured them that Carmella would have the right to keep the Paradisimo property, her birthplace, forever. This pleased both PC and Fonsilla and they agreed to sign the trust agreement.

As part of their plan to regain control of Paradisimo, Gladisa and Elsa met with Ramon several times to discuss his plans to build a commercial and shopping center on the property. They told Ramon he was like a son to them and in order to show him their gratitude they would place his name in their wills as the sole beneficiary of their estates.

Each time Carmella visited her aunts, they called Ramon. Carmella got to know Ramon and enjoyed his company. She believed that Ramon was helping her parents and her aunts. Although Carmella knew she was ten years younger than Ramon, she grew comfortable with his guidance and attention.

When Carmella turned fifteen, Ramon invited her to go to a movie with him. Although there were boys at school who asked her to go out with them, Carmella preferred to spend time with Ramon. She believed he was more mature than the boys at school and she was impressed with his ability to deal with people. PC and Fonsilla were pleased with Carmella's relationship with Ramon because they trusted him.

Gladisa and Elsa continued to plot with Ramon to build his commercial empire using the Paradisimo property and to convince Carmella it was the right thing to do despite her parents' wishes to make the property a game reserve. Ramon often spoke to Carmella about his plans to build a commercial empire. He told her that he would work with her to turn the Paradisimo property into a commercial and shopping centre. He told her he had chosen a name in honor of her, his sweet Carmella. He told her the centre would be called Candiland.

Carmella knew her parents would not approve of Ramon's idea to build a commercial and shopping centre on the Paradisimo property, but Ramon was able to convince her that her parents were old-fashioned and their ideas were out of date. Ramon told her the world was different than it had been when her parents were young. He told her the modern world needed commerce, shopping and hotels, not animals and native grass.

Carmella knew the Paradisimo property would become hers when she turned eighteen but believed she had plenty of time to decide what to do with the property. She felt she didn't need to make quick and hasty decisions.

Three weeks before her eighteenth birthday, Ramon took her out for a romantic dinner and invited her to his house. They made love for the first time, and when Ramon asked her to marry him, Carmella was ecstatic and agreed. Carmella knew that her parents trusted Ramon and would be happy to know she had decided to marry him.

Ramon said he didn't want a big wedding, just something special for the two of them. The week she turned eighteen they were married in a registry office in Hortus, with two of their friends acting as witnesses. On Ramon´s recommendation Carmella agreed to surprise her parents with the news after the wedding.

Things changed quickly after Carmella married Ramon. Ramon convinced her that they should incorporate a company, Candiland Inc. The company took control of the Paradisimo property and allowed Ramon to start building the commercial and shopping centre on the property.

PC and Fonsilla couldn't believe it when they learnt what had happened. They couldn't understand why Carmella had decided to get married without telling them and how she could let Ramon convince her to create a company to control their beloved Paradisimo. They didn't understand how Carmella could forget the beauty and value of the natural environment she had grown up with and treat Paradisimo as nothing more than a money-making venture.

Fonsilla and PC sought legal advice to see if they could undo the trust, but were told it was too late to change the trust and Carmella now had the right to make decisions about Paradisimo. When they spoke to Carmella she told her parents she had decided to let Ramon manage her business affairs and Candiland Inc. because he had more knowledge than she did in dealing with commerce and property.

Candiland Inc. held, as its main asset, the Paradisimo property. With the encouragement of Gladisa and Elsa, Ramon decided to expand his ideas to build not only a commercial and shopping center but also a recreational center and hotel. The company, Candiland Inc., would build a commercial and shopping centre, an amusement Park and the Candiland hotel. Fonsilla and PC were given a small parcel of land beside the new Candiland complex.

Unfortunately, not all went well with the Candiland project. The initial date set to open Candiland was delayed because of archaeological findings of fossils on the Paradisimo property. This meant Candiland Inc. was not able to open to the public until excavation and removal of the fossils had been completed. As well, the cost of building Candiland Hotel exceeded budget, necessitating Carmella and Ramon to make additional cash contribution to keep the project moving ahead. Gladisa and Elsa gave Carmella and Ramon the cash they needed on the condition that the hotel be re-named the Gladelsa hotel and large neon lights be installed to display the Gladelsa name. They also demanded to receive fifty-five per cent of profits made by the hotel.

A year after the Candiland Amusement Park opened, one of the amusement rides went off its rails. Two people were killed and five people were injured. Legal actions were commenced against Candiland Inc. by the families of the deceased riders and by people who were injured in the accident. The reputation of Candiland suffered and resulted in major financial losses for Candiland Inc. and the Gladelsa hotel.

Five years after Candiland Inc. was incorporated, it faced bankruptcy. Candiland Inc. was placed in the hands of a firm of accountants who acted as trustees to deal with the sale and distribution of its assets and property. Distribution of funds was made to the secured creditor banks, judgement creditors and to pay for the services of lawyers and accountants. Unfortunately, no money was left for ordinary creditors. Gladisa and Elsa found out they were ordinary creditors. Ramon had cheated them by not drafting contracts to make them secured creditors. They learnt they would not be able to recover the money they lent to Ramon and Carmella to make the cash injection nor would they be able to recover their share of profits of the Gladelsa hotel when it was making a profit. Gladisa and Elsa were outraged and plotted to destroy anything associated with Paradisimo, Ramon and Carmella.

First, they changed their wills to ensure that Ramon and Carmella would not benefit from their estates. They then decided to destroy the remaining piece of the Paradisimo property, that being the small parcel of land where Fonsilla and PC lived.

They contacted a scientist working with genetic modification to concoct a synthetic pesticide XXP designed to kill plants and trees. They hired a disgruntled student with an airplane to spray the pesticide over the Paradisimo property occupied by Fonsilla and PC. Within days the plants and trees withered and the animals left the area or died.

Their final plan was to ensure that Carmella and Ramon would never return to Candiland. They build a fire bomb and took it to the Gladelsa hotel where they ignited the bomb to burn the Candiland complex and the property of Fonsilla and PC.

Fonsilla and PC had no option but to leave their Paradisimo home. It is understood they are now destitute and living on the streets of Hortus.

Ramon and Carmella are divorced. They have both left Torcia. It is unknown where or how they are living.

Gladisa and Elsa know they lost some money but are happy with the overall result of their plot. Candiland has been destroyed and Ramon and Carmella have left their homeland.

For Gladisa and Elsa the best news was that Paradisimo has been lost forever.

The Judgement Game

1) Do you believe that Gladisa and Elsa will be punished for their crimes?

Yes ☐ No ☐

2) Who are the victims in this vignette?

_____

_____

_____

3) Who are the offenders in this vignette?

_____

_____

_____

4) What crimes do you identify in this vignette?

_____

_____

_____

5) Do you believe Fonsilla´s horse still has its´ diamond studded shoes?
Yes ☐ No ☐

WHOM CAN WE TRUST?

You will read cases of breach of trust. Breach of trust is not a criminal offence in Torcia. In Torcia, it is subject to remedies in Torcia´s civil Courts. You will be asked whether it should be made a criminal offence, and you will provide your decision about what remedy be recommended in each of the situations presented.

Case Number 1 - Bernard

Bernard granted a power of attorney to his children. The power of attorney was given to his son, Noel, and his daughter, Laurie. His intention was to facilitate banking arrangements for his children who were helping care for him.

After Bernard granted the power of attorney, Laurie withdrew $6,000 from her father's account and put it in her own account. She later transferred $79,000 from her father's account for her own use. Her father was declared incompetent one day after the second transaction.

The son, Noel, brought an action in Torcia´s civil Court. He asked for return of the money Laurie had taken from her father's account and for an accounting.

The Court ordered the removal of Laurie as an attorney, that she repay the two amounts taken from the account and that she provide an accounting.

The Judgement Game
1) Do you agree with the Court's decision?
Yes ☐ No ☐

Why or why not?

_____

_____

_____

2) Should this type of breach of trust be a criminal rather than a civil offence?

Yes ☐ No ☐

Why or why not?

_____

_____

_____

3) I want to make my own decision. It is:

_____

_____

_____

Case Number 2 - Manuel

Manuel gave Doug a power of attorney to do his banking and to pay his bills while Manuel was in the hospital. Manuel spent two months in the hospital, during which time he was seriously ill and often disoriented.

During the first month Manuel was in hospital, Doug transferred $97,000 to himself by way of five cheques, alleged to be gifts. Before Manuel died, Doug transferred to himself an additional $139,000 by way of separate cheques, again alleged to be gifts. Doug testified that Manuel wanted Doug to have all his money when he died, but that Manuel did not have time to change his will. Doug testified that all money transferred to him was intended to be gifts.

Manuel's estate sued for return of the alleged gifts and specifically alleged that Manuel did not authorize Doug to benefit himself in this manner. The estate argued that even if Manuel had given Doug authorisation to transfer the funds, Manuel did not have the mental capacity to make that authorisation.

The action was allowed. Torcia's civil Court held that because Manuel was now deceased, the testimony supporting the alleged gifts had to be convincing and unchallengeable. It found the evidence that Manuel intended to make gifts of the monies to Doug was not convincing and unchallengeable.

The Court determined Manuel could have changed his will to benefit Doug if he had wanted to. He had not, however, done so.

The Court felt no satisfactory explanation had been provided for the separate cheques written by Manuel. It noted the cheques were for odd amounts and given during the last three months of Manuel's life. The Court found Doug's evidence either to be false or, in some cases, although not proved to be completely false, lacking credibility.

Doug was ordered to repay the amounts to Manuel's estate.

The Judgement Game

1) Do you agree with the Court's decision?

Yes [   ] No [   ]

Why or why not?

_____

_____

_____

_____

2) Should this type of breach of trust be a criminal rather than a civil offence?

Yes [   ] No [   ]

Why or why not?

_____

_____

_____

3) I want to make my own decision. It is:

_____

_____

_____

Case Number 3 - Eric

Eric had suffered a serious brain injury in a motor vehicle accident that left him blind. Eric granted a power of attorney to his brother, Daryl, to use his bank accounts in order to look after him.

The power of attorney was given to Daryl with explicit instructions it could only be used under the direction of Eric. The power of attorney document had been signed by Daryl stating he agreed to act exclusively for the benefit of Eric and could not make withdrawals, sign cheques, or otherwise deal with Eric's property for Daryl's personal benefit.

During a period of eight months, Daryl committed breach of trust by making numerous unauthorized transactions for his own personal benefit without consulting or notifying Eric. The unauthorized transactions amounted to $100,000.

The unauthorized transactions included:

- withdrawals of significant amounts of cash for his own use;
- purchases of erotic videos;
- purchases of airline tickets to Rehna;
- purchase of hotel reservations and dinners in Rehna.

Eric's lawyer asked the Court to award judgement for $100,000 against Daryl and to order punitive damages of $10,000.

This application was opposed by Daryl who indicated that he deserved the money for looking after Eric.

Torcia Civil Court Judgement
The Court awarded a judgement against Daryl for $100,000. The money was ordered to be returned to Eric's account. The Court also awarded punitive costs of $10,000, as requested by Eric's lawyer.

1) Do you agree with the Court's decision?
Yes ☐ No ☐

Why or why not?

_____
_____
_____

2) Should this type of breach of trust be a criminal rather than a civil offence?
Yes ☐ No ☐

Why or why not?

_____
_____
_____

3) I want to make my own decision. It is:

_____
_____
_____

BOYS AND GIRLS IN BLUE

National News has recently learnt of a situation in which the police were investigating a domestic dispute in Colby. The dispute involved a group of people who had recently immigrated to Torcia from Loma. The police knew the people, as the police had previously had occasion to arrest members of the same family at this address in relation to other matters.

When officers arrived at the scene of the dispute, the people being investigated became aggressive and started verbally abusing the officers. The situation became violent, and police officers were alleged to have beaten residents at the house. One man was severely beaten. His right hand was injured so badly, it required complete reconstruction and his right leg had been broken when smashed against a table. The man was a musician who played the guitar professionally. He had previously recorded an album and had signed a contract to produce two more albums. Because of the injuries he sustained in the police assault, he was unable to continue his professional music career.

National News obtained information about three legal proceedings commenced because of this incident.

The Internal Police Investigation
The police members involved in the incident closed ranks and were not prepared to provide information about which officer or officers had assaulted the musician. As a result, no punishment was provided to any of the police officers involved in the incident.

The Civil Claim
A civil claim was made against the police department and the officer for the loss of the musician's income and the profits of his contracts to produce two albums. That claim was successful. There was enough information to prove, on a balance of probabilities,

that Constable X assaulted the musician. The musician received a monetary settlement for the civil assault and his loss of income claim.

The Criminal Action

Criminal charges were laid against Constable X, one of the officers who had attended at the house being investigated. Following trial, the Court found there was insufficient evidence to prove, beyond a reasonable doubt that Constable X was the officer who had assaulted the musician. Other officers would not provide evidence against Constable X, and it was only the evidence of the musician and the medical evidence of the injuries that the judge had to rely on. When asked questions by his lawyer, the musician identified Constable X as the officer who injured his hand and crushed his leg against the table. On cross-examination, however, the musician acknowledged that several officers had been holding him, including Constable X but not only Constable X. Based on this evidence the State was not successful in proving beyond a reasonable double that Constable X was responsible for the musician's injuries.

1) Provide your comments as to the results of the three legal proceedings:
The Internal Police Investigation:

_____

_____

_____

The Civil Action

_____

_____

_____

The Criminal Action

_____

_____

_____

Self-Assessment

You have the opportunity to provide a self-assessment after reading the vignettes in "Home Invasion and Breach of Trust."

Indicate how many points* you give yourself for:

1) Recognition of issues raised in the chapter. ___

2) Suggestions and comments you made. ___

3) Your role as a decision maker. ___

TOTAL: ___

*You can give yourself 0 (lowest) to 5 (highest) points.

This is a game. Remember there are no right or wrong answers.

CHAPTER 8:
IMPAIRED DRIVING OFFENCES

• • •

The following are common examples of cases involving impaired driving in Torcia. You are the decision maker for the Impaired Driving Tribunal (IDT). After each case, you are asked to make a sentencing recommendation.

Torcia wants you to provide suggestions as to what can be done to stop the carnage on the highways resulting from the problem of driving while under the influence of alcohol. You may find this information dry and repetitive but you are to treat each case as important and unique. Each case has subtle differences.

You can impose the following sentencing alternatives:

1) Impose a monetary penalty in an amount that <u>you set.</u>

2) Send the offender to jail for six months.

3) Place the offender on probation on terms that he/she attends an alcohol addiction centre.

4) Make your own decision.

In each case, you will make a decision whether or not to allow the offender to install the C-MIND machine in his or her vehicle after he or she has completed three months of the mandatory one-year license suspension.

Special Notes for You

➢ For each driving offence, there is a mandatory one-year suspension of the offender's driver's license. The offender will need to apply to IDT, write a driver's exam, and pay a fee to obtain a new license after the completion of the one-year suspension.

> ➤ The C-MIND machine when installed in the offender's vehicle allows the offender, after completing a minimum of three months of the mandatory one-year licence suspension, to drive his vehicle when he or she has not been drinking alcohol. The C-MIND machine is a complicated machine and new invention that measures the offender's breath and forwards a message to C-MIND Central. If alcohol is detected on the offender's breath, a message is sent to C-MIND Central and the driver will not be able to start his or her vehicle. It also allows C-MIND Central to read the mind of the offender to obtain information about his or her thoughts. Concerns have been raised by human rights groups that the machine breaches a citizen's right to privacy. It is, however, a choice made by Torcian citizens to agree whether or not he or she will allow C-MIND Central to read his or her thoughts. Should an offender request the machine be installed, you, the IDT decision maker, can allow the offender to install the C-Mind machine in his or her vehicle. The C-MIND machine will only be available to the offender if he or she requests it and you allow it.

LILLIAN´S CASE

Submission by Lillian's Lawyer

Lillian is a resident of the city of Reda. She has lived in Reda all of her life. She is fifty-five years old. She is married and has six children. Only one of her children still lives at home.

Lillian entered a plea of guilty to impaired driving. Lillian has no previous criminal record.

Lillian has been a member of the city council of Reda for the past three years. This is a paid position. She also provides voluntary work for the Reda annual city festival by organizing events for the festival. She indicates that her driver's license is important to her because she needs it for her job and for her many community activities.

Lillian entered a guilty plea at the first opportunity and co-operated with the police throughout their investigation. She asked me to advise you she does her best to be a good citizen.

On the day of the offence, Lillian indicates that she had been at a pool party with friends. She and her friends were drinking tequila and orange juice coolers because of the heat. One of Lillian's friends took Lillian home after the pool party. Lillian went to sleep for a couple of hours. When she woke, she needed cigarettes and decided to drive to a supermarket in Reda to buy them, never thinking she might still be impaired and should not drive.

When Lillian failed to yield at an intersection, she was stopped by police. The officer noted that Lillian smelled of alcohol and asked her to take a Breathalyzer test. The test showed the alcohol in Lillian's blood was slightly over the limit allowed by Torcia's law.

Lillian has asked me to advise you she needs her car to drive to work each day and to continue her work for the Reda annual festival. Lillian applies to install the C-MIND machine in her vehicle after her licence has been suspended for three months. Lillian has asked me to indicate that she is not concerned with a breach of her rights of privacy because she has nothing to hide from the State.

In the event Lillian is not allowed to install the C-MIND machine, she will be required to walk one kilometre back and forth to work and will not be able to continue her volunteer activities for the annual Reda festival.

Submission by Torcia's State lawyer
It is submitted that your tribunal should impose a five thousand dollar fine based on Lillian's income. The State opposes allowing Lillian to install the C-MIND machine in her vehicle. It is submitted there are no compelling reasons for Lillian to drive. She is able to walk the short distance of one kilometre back and forth to work

and it is not imperative that she provide volunteer services for the Reda annual festival this year.

The Judgement Game

1) Impose a monetary penalty in an amount that you set._$___

2) Send the offender to jail for six months.
Yes [   ] No [   ]

3) Place the offender on probation on terms that she attends an alcohol addiction centre.
Yes [   ] No [   ]

4) I want to make my own decision. It is:

_____

_____

_____

Allow the offender to install the C-MIND machine in her vehicle after she has completed three months of the mandatory one-year license suspension.
Yes [   ] No [   ]

Why or Why Not?

_____

_____

_____

LEN´S CASE

Len's Submission

I am twenty-three years old. I am married and have a five-year-old daughter. I live in the city of Jervis.

I have a job as a postal delivery driver for the company, Jervis Delivery Inc. I provide deliveries to Jervis Delivery clients throughout the city. I need my licence in order to provide services to my Jervis clients.

I know I have a drinking problem. When this offence happened, I had been under a lot of stress. My wife has cervical cancer and is required to take chemotherapy treatments. I was worried about what could happen to my wife and my family because of my wife's illness. I know that I use alcohol to avoid my problems. That is what I always do when I am faced with difficulties.

On the day of the event, I started drinking early in the morning and continued to drink all afternoon. When the bar closed, I needed to drive home. I recall, I was speeding and spinning my tires when I started my vehicle outside the bar. I wanted the world to know I was upset.

Someone must have called the police because I recall hearing a siren and seeing a police car driving towards me. I stopped my vehicle when I saw the police car. I knew that I was the one they were after.

This is the fifth time I have been charged with offences when I was driving after having too much to drink. I know I have a drinking problem. I have tried to stop drinking but nothing seems to work.

Please don´t send me to jail. If I'm sent to jail, I will lose my job. My wife and I have enough problems to deal with at the present. My wife can only work part-time because or her illness. I do not know how we will cope if I am sent to jail.

I ask you allow me to install the C-MIND programme because my work requires me to drive. I will not be able to continue my job without having the ability to drive. I´m worried, however, that the C-MIND machine can read my thoughts and I may find myself in more trouble if the Torcian police do not like what I am thinking. I do not have much choice, however, and I am willing to take the risk because I need to drive for my work obligations.

As well, I need time to pay any fine you may impose. I need at least a month to pay the fine.

Submission by Torcia's State lawyer
The State submits that Len be incarcerated for two months. His criminal record shows he has not respected Torcia's laws against drinking and driving. He has been convicted of impaired driving on four previous occasions. It is recommended he be required to take alcohol training both during the time of his incarceration and for one year after his release.

The State opposes allowing Len to install the C-MIND programme. It is submitted that your decision must show him that he must respect the law against driving while under the influence of alcohol. The State submits that Len should seek rehabilitation in prison where he can access professional alcohol addiction services.

The Judgement Game
1) Impose a monetary penalty in an amount that you set._$___

2) Send the offender to jail for six months.
Yes [   ] No [   ]

3) Place the offender on probation on terms that he attends an alcohol addiction centre.
Yes [   ] No [   ]

4) Adopt the Torcia State lawyer's recommendation that Len be incarcerated for two months and that he be required to take alcohol training both during the time of his incarceration and for one year after his release.
Yes [   ] No [   ]

5) I want to make my own decision. It is:

_____

_____

_____

Allow Len to apply to install the C-MIND machine in his vehicle after he has completed three months of the mandatory one-year license suspension.

Yes ☐ No ☐

Why or Why Not?

_____

_____

_____

GERALD´S CASE

Gerald entered a guilty plea to impaired driving.

Torcia´s State lawyer's submission

The police report shows that the offender was grossly intoxicated the evening of the offence. The offender's vehicle was stopped in response to a call reporting a car weaving across the road. When the offender exited the car, he was unable to maintain his balance and fell on the ground.

The police report indicates the offender's speech was slurred and his eyes bloodshot. The offender was held over-night at the police station and his vehicle impounded for forty-eight hours.

The State takes no position regarding the recommendation as to whether Gerald should be allowed to install the C-MIND pro-gramme in his vehicle after completing three months of the mandatory license suspension.

Gerald's Submission

I am a high school student. I will graduate from high school in eight months if I am able to finish my studies. Please don´t send me to jail because that would mean I would not finish my studies and graduate. I hope this offence will not disrupt my studies.

I have no previous criminal record. I am pleading guilty the first day I was scheduled to address this charge.

I live in a trailer park with my girlfriend and our baby. The trailer park is on the outskirts of Kata, and approximately five kilometres from my high school.

It is important for me to be able to attend my classes during the week. After I was charged with this offence, one of my friends helped me by driving me back and forth to school. I cannot keep imposing on my friend to help me. I have heard about the C-MIND machine and request you allow me to install the machine in my vehicle after I have completed three months of the mandatory license suspension. I need a car to drive to school to finish my studies. I don´t have time to worry what C-MIND Central and the State may do with my thoughts. I want to finish high school and graduate because I need my High School diploma so I can get a job to support my family and myself.

I accept responsibility for the offence. I know I should not have driven the night of this offence. The reason I drove is that I had left my girlfriend alone all day with the baby. I needed to get home to look after them.

Should you decide to award a fine, I require time to pay. I ask that you give me at least three months to pay any fine. I don't have much money.

The Judgement Game

1) Impose a monetary penalty in an amount that you set._$___
2) Send the offender to jail for six months.

Yes [ ] No [ ]

3) Place the offender on probation on terms that he attends an alcohol addiction centre.

Yes [ ] No [ ]

4) I want to make my own decision. It is:

_____

_____

_____

Allow the offender to apply to install the C-MIND machine in his vehicle after he has completed three months of the mandatory one-year license suspension.

Yes [ ] No [ ]

Why or Why Not?

_____

_____

_____

Enquiry for the Reader:

Is the objective of the C-MIND programme to stop alcohol abuse?

Yes [ ] No [ ]

Why or Why Not?

_____

_____

_____

Do you believe that the C-MIND programme is an invasion of the privacy rights of Torcian citizens?

Yes [ ] No [ ]

Why or why not?

_____

_____

_____

Self-Assessment

You have the opportunity to provide a self-assessment after reading the vignettes in "Impaired Driving Offences."

    Indicate how many points* you give yourself for:

    1) Recognition of issues raised in the chapter.   ___

    2) Suggestions and comments you made.   ___

    3) Your role as a decision maker.   ___

    TOTAL: ___

*You can give yourself 0 (lowest) to 5 (highest) points.

This is a game. Remember there are no right or wrong answers.

CHAPTER 9:
BORN BAD OR JUST A GOOD TRAINING SCHOOL

• • •

The Judgement Game asks for your responses and the punishment to be imposed for the criminal offences in these crime reports. Parable: Not everything you see is what it appears to be. Not everyone you meet is who he or she appears to be.

Remember the human mind is fragile and unpredictable, and people's actions may often be a question of circumstance. Remember, as well, the fields of psychology and psychiatry may provide insights for understanding these cases.

RICHARD

Richard escaped from a maximum-security prison in Torcia. He managed to climb over the security fence during a snowstorm. The storm had caused several sections of the highly sensitive alarm system to fail, resulting in the inability of correctional staff to see some areas of the fence. Richard was considered a highly dangerous offender, and news of his escape was broadcast across Torcia. His past crimes included a string of robberies, drug offences, the murder of a police officer during one of the robberies and another conviction for the murder of two drug dealers during a deal gone wrong.

Less than a month after his escape, Richard robbed a convenience store using a shiv (knife) made in the prison and which he had managed to take with him when he escaped. He had renewed his contact with Terry, a drug dealer he knew, and had been given some cocaine as a "welcome back" gift. Terry knew he would be paid back because he was planning to get Richard to help him distribute drugs in the high schools of Corrita. Richard had a lot of experience with that type of work and was happy to be able to get back into the drug trafficking game now that he was on the outside.

Richard was a good-looking man in his late twenties. After his escape, he decided to take advantage of his freedom and find a bar where he could drink and go dancing. His intention was to find some women who would foot the bill and with whom he could spend the night. He wanted to fulfil one of his fantasies, watching women have sex with one another. He had dreamt of that many times during his long days in jail and he wanted to turn this fantasy into reality. He found a bar and dance club in Corrita and had little difficulty persuading three women to come back to his motel with him. He knew each was hoping she would be the one he would choose to have sex with.

Richard and the three women snorted some of the cocaine that Terry had given Richard. They were all feeling good. Richard told the women he wanted to watch them make love together and he would then choose one of them for himself. The women were eager to win the competition and agreed with his idea. The women started to play with one another on the bed. An erotic evening of stroking, kissing, and snuggling ensued while Richard watched. One of the women was brought to orgasm by another woman licking her. Everyone was having a good time until one of the women started laughing.

"Stop laughing at me, you bitch," Richard screamed.

He flew at the women in a rage, brandishing the knife he had used to rob the convenience store. They had little time to react. They were together on the bed, undressed and vulnerable. As he slit their throats, he screamed at them, "You fucking cows. You won't laugh at me."

Why did Richard kill the three women? Books of psychiatry and psychology may provide information, but do they provide the complete answer? Do we dare attempt to define the mental processes of this man? What we do know is that his perversions, neuroses, and manipulation of others, combined with his fantasies, became the final chapter in the lives of these women.

What else do we know?

We know Richard had a lack of concern for his fellow human beings. He was a man who ridiculed others and treated them as objects for his personal pleasure. He had many relationships with women. While in prison, he had relationships with men both consensual and non-consensual.

Richard's prison record was lengthy. He had sold and distributed drugs both in and out of jail and had a history of committing robberies. His words to the police authorities when he was arrested were, "When they saw the knife they bawled like cows, so I decided to slaughter them like cows. I was not going to let the bitches laugh at me."

For Richard these women were objects. They were objects of pleasure. That evening, they were dispensable objects.

Richard was convicted of murder and sent to a higher-security prison than the one from which he escaped.

The Judgement Game

1) Do you believe Richard can be helped by Torcia's present legal system?

Yes ☐ No ☐

Why or why not?

_____

_____

_____

2) Do you believe Richard can be helped by Torcia's present medical system?

Yes [   ] No [   ]

Why or why not?

_____

_____

_____

3) Does the information in the report provide any information about why Richard committed the murders?

Yes [   ] No [   ]

If so, what information?

_____

_____

_____

4) What additional information do you require to help understand why Richard committed the murders?

_____

_____

_____

SUNNIE AND GLYDE

Perhaps information about their childhoods will help us find out more about the offenders Sunnie and Glyde. We are not able to enter their minds to determine whether their acts were a result of genetic makeup, their own design or the influence of others. What we are able to do is to review events during their childhood to see if we gain insight about Sunnie and Glyde and why they committed the offences they did.

Sunnie and Glyde were Mexian. They were twins. They had lived in Reda all of their lives. The children's father was a general labourer in the construction industry. The children's mother worked shifts at a bar.

The children's father had been incarcerated several times for robbery and theft of vehicles as well as for assaulting his wife, the children's mother. Sunnie's father had sexually abused her when she was three years old. After Sunnie's mother learnt of the abuse, she divorced her husband and went to live on her own with the two children.

When the children were six years old, they went joyriding. Their mother had come home from work at the bar and told them she needed to take a rest and they should play together in the kitchen before dinner.

After their mother had fallen asleep, Sunnie saw that her mother had left her car keys sitting on the kitchen table. Sunnie picked up the keys and asked Glyde if he wanted to come with her to play in the car. Sunnie knew that her mother parked her car right beside the house. The children took the keys and went to the car to play. Sunnie was bragging to Glyde that she knew how to drive a car. Glyde was impressed and asked her to teach him to drive.

A neighbour called the police when he saw Sunnie driving the car down the street with her brother sitting beside her. He could not believe his eyes. He said that he had shouted at the girl to stop but the she just kept driving. The car careened into two other vehicles before it hit an electrical pylon where it stalled. Neither Sunnie nor Glyde were injured but their mother's car and the two vehicles that had been sideswiped were damaged.

When the police officer questioned the children, Glyde told the police officer, "Sunnie was teaching me how to drive." Sunnie's comment to the officer when he asked why she had taken the car was, "It's fun to do bad things."

The police officer took the children home. By that time, their mother was awake and had seen that her car was missing. She had gone around the neighbourhood asking if anyone had seen her children and her car. She told the officer that she thought some-one had accosted the children and stolen her car.

The police officer who investigated the incident did not lay charges against Sunnie and Glyde because of their ages but laid a charge of criminal endangerment against their mother for leaving Sunnie and Glyde unattended.

After the police left, Sunnie received a beating from her mother. Glyde looked on hoping he would be spared. He wasn't spared and received an equally severe beating.

The next event of note took place when the children were ten years old. It was alleged that the children had sexually molested a girl at school. The girl, Roxanne, told a boy at school about a game her classmate Sunnie had shown her. The game was called "lollipop." Players had to pull their pants down and play with each other's private parts. Roxanne wanted the boy to play the game with her. The boy refused to play the game but told his teacher who started an investigation.

The school had its social worker interview Sunnie and Glyde´s mother as well as Sunnie and Glyde regarding the allegation. The children's mother told the social worker that Sunnie and Glyde were good children and would not have played a game like that. When questioned by the social worker, both Sunnie and Glyde denied having played the game with Roxanne.

Glyde told the social worker that he and his sister were a team. He said "we look after one another. I do what Sunnie tells me to do because she is smarter than I am." He told the social worker that Roxanne didn´t like him or Sunnie because they were Mex-ian.

Sunnie told the social worker that she was bigger and stronger than Glyde and often had to defend Glyde from bigger boys and girls at school who were threatening to beat him up because he was Mexian. She also said that the children at school, including Roxanne, picked on her and Glyde. Sunnie said her mother told her the community was racist against Mexian people and she would just have to get used to it. Sunnie told the social worker that Roxanne was not telling the truth. She said Roxanne wanted to cause problems for Sunnie and Glyde so they would be kicked out of school

The social worker recommended the family see a psychologist. The children's mother told the social worker, "Me and my kids don't need to see a shrink. I don't think anything happened to that Roxanne girl. The children at school do not treat my children as equals because we are Mexian."

No further action was taken by the school. The social worker determined there was insufficient evidence against Sunnie and Glyde to show that either child had sexually molested Roxanne.

When Sunnie and Glyde were seventeen, they decided to rob a chain of jewellery stores, the Goldie stores. News broadcasts about the robberies were extensive throughout Reda and neighbouring cities. A police search for Sunnie and Glyde was started.

It did not take long before Sunnie and Glyde were apprehended and charged. After retaining legal counsel, they entered guilty pleas to five counts of robbery. The judge who sentenced them said she wanted to make an example of the children to deter them and others from this type of offence. Sunnie was given a sentence of incarceration of twenty-four months in a young offenders centre for girls and Glyde was given a sentence of incarceration for thirteen months in a young offenders centre for boys.

When the judge gave her sentence, she indicated that her review of the police report led her to conclude that Sunnie was the leader and had convinced Glyde to follow her but both offenders needed to learn a lesson. Her judgement went on to say: "Not only do we need to know our streets are safe, but also that daily activities such as shopping can be undertaken without fear from local hooligans like Sunnie and Glyde. I needed to provide a sentence that reflects community values and punishes people who decide to take advantage of our businesses."

When Sunnie and Glyde were twenty they were subjects of a police investigation for a robbery and kidnapping in the North Reda area. A thirty-year-old woman reported being robbed and kidnapped at three in the morning when she was walking along Robson Street. She said a Mexian man and woman, meeting the description of Sunnie and Glyde, forced her into their vehicle, stole her money and dropped her off a short time later. The victim told the police that when she was stopped, the female assailant said:

"Welcome to our stagecoach, lady. Hand us your wallet. We are collecting money for a good cause."

Following investigation by police, Sunnie and Glyde were charged with robbery and kidnapping. They both entered guilty pleas. No sentence has been made for this offence. You are asked for your comments on the sentences imposed for the Goldie robberies and the Stagecoach robbery and kidnapping.

The Judgement Game

1) Does the information in the report provide any information about why Sunnie and Glyde committed the Goldie robbery offences?

Yes [   ] No [   ]

What information?

_____

_____

_____

2) Do you believe the judge had any alternative but to send Sunnie and Glyde to jail for the Goldie robbery offences?
Yes ☐ No ☐

Why or why not?

_____
_____
_____

3) What sentence would you recommend be imposed on Sunnie for the Stagecoach robbery and kidnapping?
Absolute Discharge [17]____
Conditional Discharge [18]____

If the discharge were conditional, what conditions would you impose?

_____
_____
_____

Fine ____
Probation with conditions that she attends counselling for violence against others____
Jail ____
I want to impose my own sentence. It is:

_____
_____
_____

17 An absolute discharge means the offender will go free with only a written warning from the Court.
18 A conditional discharge means the offender will be released on the conditions you, the decision maker, set.

4) What sentence would you recommend be imposed on Glyde for the Stagecoach robbery and kidnapping?

Absolute Discharge[19]___

Conditional Discharge [20]___

If the discharge were conditional, what conditions would you impose?

_____

_____

_____

Fine ___

Probation with conditions that he attends counselling for violence against others ___

Jail ___

I want to impose my own sentence. It is:

_____

_____

_____

5) Share your ideas about what steps can be taken to help stop Sunnie and Glyde from committing further offences.

_____

_____

_____

---

19 An absolute discharge means the offender will go free with only a written warning from the Court.

20 A conditional discharge means the offender will be released on the conditions that you, the decision-maker, set.

FACING THE PAROLE BOARD

Background Information for the Parole Board Hearing

Brian was given a sentence of life imprisonment for two murders that he committed. The law of Torcia gave Brian the right to apply to the parole board to allow him to live in a halfway house in the community after serving twenty years of his sentence. Brian has commenced this application to be released on parole to allow him to live in a halfway house for the next five years.

You are one of the three members of Torcia's parole board. You are asked to review the following written material and to make a decision about Brian's release. Other members of the parole board will be asked to do the same. The final decision will be based on the majority of the three responses received. You will not know the final decision but will know that you have contributed to the decision making process.

Brian's Written Statement to the Parole Board

The crime happened when I was seventeen years old. I am now thirty-seven years old. I have spent much of my life in prison but ask you to give me a second chance. I know what I did was wrong. My life was a mess when I was seventeen. I was a rebel who wouldn't listen to others. I was addicted to alcohol and cocaine.

I have been told that one cannot learn how to live in freedom when in a state of captivity, but have tried my best to prove this statement wrong. I believe that even though I have been in jail for the past twenty years, I have learnt how to handle my problems without resorting to drugs or violence. I ask you to provide me the opportunity to continue my life outside the prison walls and to show what I have learnt about others and myself. I have learnt how to deal with my personal disabilities, being my addiction to drugs and my lack of self-confidence. I want to make up for what I did by helping people learn how to deal with their physical disabilities. I would like the opportunity to become a contributing member of Torcian society.

I will tell you about the night my life fell apart, the night I murdered my parents. On the night of the murder, I had gone to the local town, Colby, fifteen kilometres from my parents' farm. I'd gone to a party in Colby. My girlfriend, Fiona, asked me if I wanted to do some cocaine with her at the party. I'd been using coke for some time. I'd smoked it and sniffed it, but had never injected it. My friends told me freebasing or injecting the coke would produce more profound effects. I wanted to impress Fiona so I told her, "Let's go for it. No problem, as long as I get home early enough to milk the cows for my parents."

I remember Fiona laughed at me. "Still a mommy's boy, I see. Don't worry; we'll make sure you get home in time to milk Bossy."

Fiona's comment about my being a "mommy's boy" angered me and made me more determined to use the drug to lighten up. I gave Fiona my arm and told her to give me the injection. I trusted her to do this for me because I was nervous with needles and I knew she was a nurse's aide at the Colby hospital.

I remember the psychedelic colours and the feeling of detachment from my body that the drug caused. I remember the voice in my head. The voice was mine but not mine. The voice was telling me to milk the cows and then started screaming at me to milk the cows. There was laughter all around me. The voice told me to pick up the axe. That's all I remember until I woke up and saw what I had done. I had split my parents' heads open with the axe.

Psychologist's Report to the Parole Board – Dr. David Clifford

Brian has been in jail since the age of seventeen. He is the eldest child in a family of three children. There was a period of seven years between Brian's birth and the birth of the twins, his brother and sister. On the day of the murder, Brian's siblings were not home but away at children's camp. Brian was seventeen years old. His brother and sister were ten.

He stated that his mother was thirty-six when the twins were born. According to Brian, his mother suffered postpartum depression following the birth of the twins. When I questioned him about where he learnt of that diagnosis, Brian indicated that his mother's hospital had shared the information with his father who, in turn, shared it with Brian. The information had been provided when Brian's mother left the hospital.

Brian told me his mother was very depressed when she came home with the twins. He said she had trouble sleeping and wanted to be left alone and he overheard her tell his father she was too old to look after babies and didn't want the twins.

Brian indicated that after his mother came home from the hospital, she would do little more than give the twins their milk and change their diapers. Brian told me he'd tried to play with the babies and to give them the love and care he knew his mother wasn't able to give them.

Brian told me that his father was a strong and forceful man who was devoted to his wife and to Brian. Brian said that although he was sure his father loved the twins; he believed his father had little time for the twins because of having to look after his wife, his farm, and his cattle business. Brian indicated he had tried to help his parents by taking on the responsibility of milking the cows.

My review of the psychological and psychiatric reports filed at the time of Brian's incarceration indicates that the murder appears to be an isolated incident. Based on self-reports to police, Brian was addicted to cocaine. This is supported by the withdrawal symptoms recorded by the prison hospital following his incarceration. The psychiatric report on file suggests that the intensity of the drug taken intravenously resulted in his being unable to suppress his feelings of guilt and violence. The report indicated he'd been forging his father's signature on cheques and stealing money from his father's bank account to support his cocaine habit. One report indicated that his father had become aware of the thefts prior to the murder.

Brian told me this mother's sister tried to sexually assault him when he was sixteen. He said this was the first time he had told anybody about that incident. He said he'd rejected her advances but didn't tell anyone, because he didn't want his mother to find out what her sister had done. I reviewed earlier prison reports and there was no mention of that incident. It is, therefore, uncorroborated information provided by Brian. The aunt is now deceased. I am not prepared to opine as to whether this alleged sexual assault on Brian by his aunt took place or has any relevance to the murder. The incident happened over twenty years ago; there is no independent evidence of the assault, and there are no people who can verify the event.

In response to my questions about his relationship with his parents, he replied, "My parents loved me and I loved them. I felt horrible when I betrayed my parents." Brian has one photograph of his parents taken at their wedding.

In response to my questions about his siblings, he replied, "I tried to take care of them when they were babies. Since the murder, I haven't had any contact with them. They were put in foster homes because my father had no siblings and my mother only had one sister who was not willing to look after the twins." Brian has no photographs of his siblings.

Brian said he had never met his grandparents and only seen pictures of them. He said that his father's parents looked like they were happy people because they had been smiling in the photos he had been shown. He had seen only one photo of his mother's parents. He said the photo he saw showed them standing outside a sod house. He had no recollection of their faces.

No incidents of violence have been recorded during Brian's incarceration.

Social Worker's Report to the Parole Board- Pamela Sisson
This report is written for the purpose of Brian's application for parole. My report will focus on my review of the police report filed

at the time of Brian's incarceration, prison reports filed during his incarceration and my interviews with Brian.

My review of the police report of Constable Riddick of the Colby Detachment showed:

- Call to Colby Detachment from Brian XXX 5:45 a.m.
- Attendance at the XXX farmstead and house 6:10 a.m.
- Found two dead bodies positively identified as Mr and Mrs XXX by the suspect, Brian XXX.
- An axe was found beside the bodies of Mr and Mrs XXX. Forensic examination of the axe showed the fingerprints of Brian XXX.
- Statement of Brian XXX indicating he had been given an intravenous injection believed to be cocaine at a party in Colby. Suspect was unclear about how or at what time he got home.
- Brian XXX refused to provide the name of the person who injected the drug. Independent information was obtained to show that person was Fiona Burdak. No action was taken against Fiona Burdak.
- Brian XXX was placed under arrest for murder.

My review of prison records showed:

- Brian finished high school in prison. He was a student of average intelligence, but very uncertain about himself when he entered prison. He kept to himself as much as possible for the first year of his incarceration. He read, watched television, attended the gym, but had little interaction with other prisoners except as required for his work at the prison.
- After five years of incarceration, Brian took on a more active role. He helped organise games for the annual

prison Disabled Athletes Olympics event. He continued assisting with this activity for ten years.

Brian has friends in prison, both correctional officers and fellow inmates. He is, however, a loner and likes to spend time on his own. He told me he wants to help others in order to make up for the things he has done. In the interview with me he stated, "It has been so many years now since the murder happened. I have no contact with people from Colby. They have erased me from their lives, and I am happy to have been erased."

There are no reports that Brian has exhibited violent behaviour during his time in prison. Brian has successfully completed several courses while at the prison: drug and alcohol addiction training, communication skills and sport therapy.

In the event he receives parole to attend a halfway house, he indicated that he plans to enrol in sports therapy courses and seek qualification as a sports therapist for disabled athletes. He has researched grants available for prisoners so he can apply to take these courses.

The Judgement Game

1) Does the information in the report provide any information about why Brian committed the offence?

Yes ☐ No ☐

What information?

_____

_____

_____

2) Based on the information set out, are you prepared to grant Brian his request to be released from prison to a halfway house?

Yes [ ] No [ ]

Why or why not?

_____

_____

_____

3) If released to a halfway house, should he be released?
    (a) without any conditions?
Yes [ ] No [ ]

Why or why not?

_____

_____

_____

    (b) on the condition he report to a probation officer on a monthly basis for two years.
Yes [ ] No [ ]

Why or why not?

_____

_____

_____

    (c) on the condition he report to a probation officer on a monthly basis for one year?
Yes [ ] No [ ]

Why or why not?

_____

_____

_____

GUILT BY ASSOCIATION

Motorcycles and drugs led to Bill's incarceration. He had arranged to meet his friend, Pretty Boy, one evening to discuss buying a new Harley-Davidson. Pretty Boy told Bill he was planning to pick up money from Hank, the contact person for a local group of street kids to whom Pretty Boy had sold some drugs. Bill agreed to go with Pretty Boy to act as a lookout while Pretty Boy picked up the money.

A party was going on when Pretty Boy and Bill arrived at Hank's house. Bill remained outside while Pretty Boy went to the house to find Hank.

Hank met Pretty Boy at the door. "Come in and join the party, we've got lots of women, drugs, and alcohol. That should make up for the rest of the money we owe you."

Pretty Boy had no interest in joining the party. He wanted his money. He knew it was not a good time to talk business, but he decided he couldn't let Hank take advantage of him, and he pressed Hank for the money that was owed, fifteen hundred dollars.

"You can't fuck with me, I want my money," Pretty Boy said. "I'll give you an hour!" Pretty Boy held out the sawed-off shotgun he brought with him, thinking it would show Hank he meant business. Words were, however, lost on Hank and the crowd of punks behind the door.

Dan, one of the boys, high on drugs, brought out a knife and advanced towards Pretty Boy. "Think you can scare us, you shit-faced son of a bitch?"

A confrontation resulted. Bill ran in from the street when he saw the problem at the door. Dan didn't stop his advance, and Pretty Boy had no choice but to shoot. Blood and screams quickly put an end to the party, with Pretty Boy and Bill retreating to their motorbikes to get away.

Pretty Boy and Bill were both charged with first-degree murder. Following a jury trial, Pretty Boy was found guilty. Bill was found to be Pretty Boy's accomplice. Both Bill and Pretty Boy were sentenced to life imprisonment.

Bill exhausted his appeals without success.

The Judgement Game

1) Should Bill spend the rest of his life in jail for agreeing to act as a lookout for a friend?

_____

_____

_____

2) Should Torcia have a provision to allow offenders who are sentenced to life imprisonment apply for parole? [21]

Yes ☐

No ☐

If so, after how many years?

10 years ___

15 years ___

20 years ___

3) What do you believe an appropriate sentence for Bill's involvement in this offence would be and why?

_____

_____

_____

LAURA'S LESSON

Laura was found hanged in her cell

Tape Recording Found in Laura's Cell

My mother taught me when I was a baby, "He's no good. He's a drunk."

---

21 Torcia presently allows offenders sentenced to life imprisonment to apply for parole after twenty years.

She used repetition. "He's a drunk. He's ruining my life."

I was too young to understand what I was hearing, but, I listened.

Mother's repetition went on. "I work so hard. I work so hard all day and he drinks. He's no good. He's a drunk."

When I went to school, the other children told me, "Your father is a drunk. He's a no good drunk."

Stuart, my husband, was an alcoholic. Why did I marry an alcoholic? Comfort perhaps; I was familiar with the territory. It was a comfortable place.

Stuart and I built a housing empire together before Stuart's alcohol problem became out of control. My husband became abusive to me, shouting and waving his fists at me on every issue on which I didn't agree with him.

I tried to get Stuart to go for alcohol counselling. I realized he needed help. I spoke to him about the importance of getting help with his drinking problem and gave him a telephone book containing the number for Alcohol Assistance Anon (AAA). I told him, "You are an adult. You are old enough to make your own decisions, but you need help with your drinking problem." He didn't go to AAA.

He told me he was not an alcoholic and I should leave him alone. He just wanted to brag to his friends about our housing empire and keep drinking. Drinking and money had become his world. I knew I couldn't change him.

I remembered mother's messages. "He's a drunk. He's not worth saving."

I'd listened. I'd learnt.

The second message also used repetition, "Don't drink and Drive". The message was on the radio, the television and posted throughout the community. It was posted everywhere.

I knew that Stuart was drinking and driving. I didn't know what to do to stop him. I bought a magnetic sticker and placed it on the fridge. It was a beacon to alert him, "Don't drink and drive"! I watered down his bottles of whiskey.

I remember the night well. Stuart asked me to take him to the liquor store. I knew he only wanted to buy more whiskey; he was a drunk, an alcoholic. I was busy and told him I couldn't take him.

Stuart had not listened to the message. He took the car. He was in an accident. They told me it was a head on collision. Stuart was killed. He killed two people when he ran into their car.

They said it was my fault. How could they say it was my fault? I had learnt my lesson well; he was a drunk, he was an alcoholic, he wasn't worth saving."

The judge said I was responsible for the death of my husband and the two people he hit. The judge said it was my responsibility to stop Stuart from going out to buy more whiskey. How could it be my responsibility?

The Court convicted me of criminal negligence causing death. They sent me to jail.

I learnt my lesson. I don't want to learn more.´

The Judgement Game

1) Does the information in the report provide any information about why Laura committed suicide?

Yes ☐ No ☐

What information?

_____

_____

_____

2) Should Laura have been convicted of criminal negligence causing death?

Yes ☐ No ☐

Why or why not?

_____

Self-Assessment

You have the opportunity to provide a self-assessment after reading the vignettes in "Born Bad or Just a Good Training School"?

    Indicate how many points* you give yourself for:

    1) Recognition of issues raised in the chapter.   ___

    2) Suggestions and comments you made.   ___

    3) Your role as a decision maker.   ___

    TOTAL: ___

*You can give yourself 0 (lowest) to 5 (highest) points.
This is a game. Remember there are no right or wrong answers.

CHAPTER 10:
DEFINING THE PROBLEMS

•   •   •

EVERY PARENT´S NIGHTMARE

National News Report

Torcian society is in shock after the violent sexual assault and murder of a thirteen-year-old girl at Woodhouse School. A seventeen-year-old boy has been charged with aggravated sexual assault and murder for this incident. Five thousand people from the town of Cabar, where the school is located, marched in the streets to honour the young girl, Anna Duncan. The people called on the Torcian state to review its juvenile justice system.

Anna Duncan was a ninth grade student at Woodhouse, a private boarding school approximately two hundred kilometres from the Duncan's home in Leids. Anna was an only child and her parents' pride and joy. Students from Anna's school indicated she was a friendly and outgoing girl.

Anna's parents are both doctors. They told us they enrolled Anna in a mixed school setting due to Woodhouse´s reputation for providing students with an open and liberal education.

The murder suspect, Jeremy X, is from Salim. His father is a high school teacher, his mother an accountant. He has two younger sisters, ten and eleven years old.

National News learned that the alleged offender, Jeremy X, was under judicial supervision for another offence involving the alleged sexual assault of a twelve year old girl two years ago and that his upcoming trial for that offence has been scheduled.

The spokesperson for Woodhouse indicated that the school was shocked by this incident and was working with the police service in its investigation. She indicated that the school would be assisting the Duncan family in coping with this tragedy.

Recollections of Dr. Les Duncan

I had just returned from my rounds at the hospital when I received the call from the police. The officer asked if he might come by our house in the next hour to speak to my wife and me about our daughter, Anna. I told him we were both home and he could come by.

I couldn't imagine why he wanted to talk to us about Anna. She was at school. We had taken her to school three weeks earlier and had been receiving weekly messages from her to tell us how she was doing. Her message on the weekend said she was well and keeping busy with her new friends.

Within the hour, two police officers arrived at our house. It didn't take long for them to break the bad news: "We are sorry to have to tell you this, but…"

My heart fell. What could be wrong?

The officer continued, "Anna has met an untimely death." He paused as if waiting for me to say something.

"No, Anna is at school," I replied.

The second officer took over. "We will share with you what we know about the incident. We don't know everything yet. Our office is continuing its investigation. We will tell you what we know."

The officer explained to us that Anna's school bag had been found by a man near the main gate of the school. The officer said there was no doubt the school bag was Anna's. It contained her wallet and camera. The officer indicated that the man who found the school bag said it had been left in plain sight at the entrance of the school, as if someone had left it there intending it to be found.

The first officer told us that a seventeen-year-old boy, Jeremy X, had been placed in custody and was a suspect in Anna's murder. He said photos on the camera left no doubt about Anna's death, but the police had not yet found her body. Although the police shared some of the details about their investigation with us, they were hesitant to say too much until charges had been brought against the boy.

I was in shock. "No, it can't be Anna. I don't believe what you are telling us." I kept repeating, "It isn't true. Anna is at school."

My wife, Lori was crying and holding my hand as the police prepared to leave. It was all too fast, too brutal, and too cold. Before they left, one of the officers gave us a card with a twenty-four hour telephone number for the victim services unit that could be called for assistance. With no more explanation, they left us alone in our despair.

Our Anna murdered. It couldn't be true.

We learnt quickly it was true. The first telephone call was from the school. "We regret to inform you, Dr. Duncan, of an incident that happened this morning involving your daughter. The police are presently investigating what happened."

The next call was from our local radio station. "Dr. Duncan, we are very sorry to hear...."

Then, a call from the national television station. "Dr. Duncan, our condolences to you and your wife. We are sorry to hear about your daughter's death. We assume the police have told you a suspect has been placed in custody. We understand it is a boy from her school."

The messages blurred one into another. My head was spinning. Lori was trying to hold herself together.

I wanted to scream, "Leave me alone! I have to find Anna."

I didn't scream. I didn't break down.

Our poor little girl. What happened?

Unfortunately, after the police visit and the telephone calls, the message was clear. Anna had been murdered by a boy from

Woodhouse School. Anna, our daughter, was lost to us forever. Our lives will never be the same.

The day following the incident, Lori and I were asked to attend the police station to receive further information about our daughter's death. We were told Anna had gone to the forest area near the school with a seventeen-year-old boy named Jeremy X.

Anna's school bag and camera had been found at the main school gate by a Mr Stubbs, who was visiting the school to meet his son. That gate led directly to the forest trail, the forest where the boy had taken Anna. The boy told the police Anna had agreed to go with him to look for magic mushrooms. The police indicated his story was verified by the photos on Anna's camera.

Why would she have gone with this boy? Anna was thirteen. She was too young to go alone with the boy. She was too young to know about magic mushrooms.

When the police looked at the photos on the camera, they found a video recording revealing a sordid event of horror and violence. The images on the camera showed what had taken place the day of Anna's murder and provided sufficient evidence to have Jeremy X placed in custody.

Although it would have been easy for anyone to erase the photos that had been taken, the police told me the photos were in their original state. They were gruesome. It appears Jeremy X wanted the world to have a video recording of the murder. He produced and directed his own horror movie.

The video recording showed what had happened to Anna. It showed her gagged and tied to a tree. It showed her bruised face and the blood that had flowed from her groin when the murderer inserted metal instruments in her vagina. I may be a doctor, but I am also Anna's father. The video was vile and sickening. I was appalled by the recording I couldn't bear to see it.

Anna had been killed by a monster. Our precious little girl had been beaten and violated by a monster.

Disclosure Report:

This disclosure report summarizes information from the justice department and attaches reports containing information obtained from the education and health departments.

Torcia is a society with distinct boundaries between its education, justice, and health systems. Each system operates as a separate department and as an independent entity. Each department reports independently to Torcian State authorities.

The departments have their own codes of conduct based on the norms of Torcian society: life, liberty, and security of the person. Torcia also has established codes of conduct to respect freedom of speech, religion, gender equality and privacy.

The norm for sharing information between the three systems is based on a "need to know" basis, rather than automatic disclosure. That requires the system seeking information to show why and for what purpose the information is required. Information is shared on an ongoing basis between the three systems, but the paper trial can often be long and slow.

Torcia respects an individual's right to privacy. Release of private information requires written authority from the person whose rights are affected or a Court order for the release of specified information based on public interest.

Justice Department Information

Jeremy X provided information to the police about where Anna's body was located. Following the police investigation of the offence, Jeremy X was charged with two offences: aggravated sexual assault and murder.

Jeremy X's childhood was uneventful until he became addicted to drugs at the age of thirteen. Two years ago, Jeremy X was arrested and charged with sexual assault of a twelve-year-old girl. It is alleged he had taken her to a park, gagged her, and tied her to a tree with the intention to violate her sexually. His intention to do her harm was interrupted by a telephone call from his mother telling him to come home to deal with a family emergency. That stopped Jeremy X's assault. The girl's parents reported the incident to the police and Jeremy X was charged with the offence of sexual assault causing bodily harm.

Due to the gravity of that offence against the twelve-year-old girl, Jeremy X was held in custody for four months before his indictment. He entered a plea of not guilty, his trial date was scheduled and his release conditions were established.

Reports used by the judge in establishing the release conditions had been prepared by a psychologist and psychiatrist. Both reports suggested Jeremy X be removed from the area where the offence had occurred and that he be followed by the same two medical professionals prior to his trial. The reports indicated Jeremy X was not considered a danger to society and could be reintegrated in an ordinary school. This required Jeremy X´s family to look for a school outside the region where they lived.

Jeremy X had a criminal record for possession of hashish and cocaine. When sentenced for those offences he had been required to complete alcohol and drug addiction courses. There is no information on file to show whether he completed those courses.

Police dealing with the offence committed two years ago collected information from Jeremy X´s personal computer showing he had been a frequent visitor to demonic worship websites. That information was not shared with Woodhouse School but kept in the Justice Department file for use at trial for that offence.

Woodhouse School was aware that Jeremy X was under judicial supervision. The school was not made aware of details of the alleged offence involving the twelve-year-old girl or the roles and reports of the psychiatrist and psychologist who were following Jeremy X´s progress.

Education Department Information

At the time of Anna's murder, Woodhouse School was populated with fifteen hundred students from grades seven to twelve. Jeremy X was in grade eleven, and Anna Duncan in grade nine.

A school report showed that a month before the attack against Anna, Jeremy X and several other boys appeared before the school's internal administration board charged with inappropriate behaviour towards girls at the school. Verbal abuse had been witnessed by a teacher who saw the boys following a group of girls and chanting, "puss, puss, puss." The report records Jeremy X as the ringleader of the group of boys. Surveillance tapes also record the boys following the girls in the schoolyard.

Woodhouse's psychology department provided a report from its school psychologist, Dr. Bauer. The Bauer report stated the following:

Jeremy X is an adolescent boy who is having difficulty in his relationships with girls. He is finding it hard to affirm his capacity for seduction of the opposite sex, with the result that he becomes overly aggressive with girls. This is considered a normal stage of adolescent behaviour; however, in Jeremy X's case it should be monitored and checked. The school should provide healthy opportunities for Jeremy X to express himself without being pushed to violence in his interaction with the opposite sex. I am of the opinion that outlets such as sport or physical activities will assist in healthy development of his interaction with girls so he can be successfully reintegrated in the school system.

Jeremy X is seen to be an introvert, spending long hours playing video games and watching movies on his computer.

The Bauer report speaks of interviews with teachers at Woodhouse who provided contradictory reports about Jeremy X. One teacher reported that Jeremy X was a pathological liar, telling teachers and other students completely fabricated stories. The teacher reports that Jeremy X said he had lived in Poland for several years. The teacher checked this story with Jeremy X's mother who indicated Jeremy X had lived in Torcia his entire life and the story about Poland was completely fabricated. A second teacher reported that Jeremy X was a polite boy, gifted with computers and in the area of theatre. He indicated that Jeremy X liked to invent stories, which, in his opinion, showed a boy with a creative mind.

Health Care Department Information

Woodhouse Heath Care records show each time Jeremy X attended the health-care facility seeking medical assistance. These reports contain self-reported information recording his sexual activity. The reports indicate he had been sexually active with a boy and a girl at the school. Health care records show that Jeremy X attended the heath-care facility at Woodhouse and had been prescribed medication for genital herpes. This information was considered private and not shared either with Dr. Bauer or with the Justice Department.

Dr. Les Duncan provided the following letter to the National News desk.

I have been having nightmares since the police gave me news of Anna's murder.

Nothing seems to stop the nightmares. Every night I see her gagged and tied to the tree. Her lips are bleeding. She is screaming. A man is approaching her with knives. I want to run to her, but I can't move.

There is a group of parents standing around her. I see fear in their eyes. I wake up covered in sweat. I am awake but the nightmare continues.

Why did Torcia's justice system and the school fail to keep our little girl safe?

Please help me stop the nightmare!

The Judgement Game

You are asked to provide ideas to help Torcia reshape its education and criminal justice system.

1) Based on this vignette, what problems do you identify with Torcia's education system?

_____

_____

_____

2) Based on this vignette, has Torcia's criminal justice system become too specialised?

Yes ☐ No ☐

Why or Why Not?

_____

_____

_____

3) Based on this vignette, what did the criminal justice system do or not do that contributed to Jeremy X's offences?

_____

_____

_____

4) Based on the information provided, were the medical professionals, the psychiatrists and psychologists able to identify Jeremy X's problems?

_____

_____

_____

5) Does Torcia provide adequate communication between its education system, criminal justice system, and health departments?

_____

_____

_____

RONNIE X

Ronnie X is one of Torcia's *New Age* criminals. His physical appearance was distinct and memorable, but his crimes were all too common, crimes of theft.

Ronnie X´s black hair was slicked back with gel. He wore sleeveless T-shirts, tight jeans, a leather jacket and boots that made him look more like the television character, Fonzie, than like an adolescent schoolchild. He also adopted Fonzie mannerisms to show he was "cool".

Ronnie X was from a middle-class background. His parents did their best to provide him with his basic needs. They did not have money to buy him the latest fashions, gadgets and electronic "toys". Ronnie X wanted items he saw advertised in Torcia's newspapers and on television. He wanted bicycles, sportswear and state of the art telephones and electronic gadgets. Unfortunately, Ronnie X did not have the funds to acquire these items legally.

The first time Ronnie X and his parents attended the lawyer's office, Ronnie X had stolen a bicycle. Ronnie X was thirteen years old at that time. Ronnie X's parents were upset that their son had stolen a bicycle from a store in his own neighbourhood. Ronnie X acknowledged he shouldn't have stolen the bicycle. His comment to the lawyer, "I know I was "wrrrooooogh"!

He asked the lawyer if the Court would send him to jail. Ronnie X seemed genuinely afraid that he would be sent to jail.

The lawyer knew this was Ronnie X´s first offence and it would be next to impossible that Ronnie X would be sent to jail. The lawyer told him it was unlikely he would be sent to jail. The lawyer said he would do his best to obtain a good sentence for Ronnie X. When they attended Court, the judge gave Ronnie X a stern warning and sent him home.

Eight months later Ronnie X was back at the lawyer's office. This time he had stolen sports trainers, the latest Ebox on the market. He told the lawyer he thought the shoes were cool and wanted new shoes to impress his friends. His parents were with him at the interview. Ronnie X´s comment to the lawyer in front of his parents was, "Harvey´s Sports Shop makes loads of money. They didn't need the joggers and I did, Aaaaeeyyy"!

Ronnie X´s parents said they did not know what to do with Ronnie X and hoped he would grow out of this stage. They said that Ronnie X was normally a good boy, but had fallen in with bad kids at school. The lawyer knew that Ronnie X was feeding his parents a line because the State's disclosure package for the offence did not show other people being involved in the offence. Ronnie X had been acting on this own.

After his parents had left the office Ronnie X decided to share his view of the young offenders system with the lawyer "Whoa, you need to lighten up. I talked to my friends and they gave me the scoop. The judges won't send me to jail"!

The lawyer saw that Ronnie X´s attitude had changed. He had become defiant and seemed to have lost respect for the law. Ronnie X went on to tell the lawyer what he thought of the system: "It´s a joke. We all know that! The system is Wrongamùndo! Even if I rob a bank, I'll be given a short sentence. I didn't rob a bank, so, lighten up"!

The lawyer responded by telling Ronnie X that unless he stopped breaking the law, there would be a time when the Court would have no option but to send him to jail. Ronnie X laughed and replied, "You are a good lawyer, and you won't let them send me to jail."

Ronnie X was back in the lawyer's office like clockwork, every eight months. The lawyer obtained the lightest sentences possible each time he returned. After the initial warning, Ronnie X received an absolute discharge, a conditional discharge, a small fine, a larger fine and finally probation.

Ronnie X breached his probation order with yet another theft. He had stolen the latest brand of cellular telephone from a department store. The lawyer told him that this time he was likely to be sent to jail. Ronnie X laughed.

"No problemo; I hear that the young offenders centres are like the Hilton."

For the offences of breach of probation and theft of the cellular phone, Ronnie X was given an open jail sentence of fifteen days. That meant he would check in at the young offender's centre every evening, sleep at the centre and be given breakfast in the morning before being released to attend school during the day. He would return to the centre for dinner, sleep at the centre and continue that routine for fifteen days.

The judicial system had become a game for Ronnie X. The lawyer realised that he was doing little to help Ronnie X by obtaining light sentences, but he also knew that was his job.

The Judgement Game

The criminal justice system of Torcia asks you to provide your ideas to build a more effective system to deal with young offenders.

1) What can be done in the home?

_____

_____

_____

2) What can be done in the schools?

_____

_____

_____

3) What can police do?

_____

_____

_____

4) What can lawyers do?

_____

_____

_____

5) What can the Courts do?

_____

_____

_____

6) What can young offender's centres do?

_____

_____

_____

7) What can the media do?

_____

_____

_____

8) Do Torcia's education, police, legal and Court systems provide a coordinated approach in dealing with offences committed by young offenders?

Yes [   ] No [   ]

_____

_____

_____

TIME TRAVEL WITH DAMIENS

Time Travel With Damiens Commences

It is 1757. Following his discharge from the Torcian army, Damiens became a domestic servant at the college of Goldsuits in Rehna. He had been discharged from this position and from several other employments due to alleged misconduct.

Damiens planned to assassinate the then reigning king of Torcia for the king's inability to control the State and its bureaucrats. Damiens assassination attempt failed. He was apprehended immediately after the incident and made no attempt to escape. His trial was swift.

Following a hearing by Torcia's Congress, Damiens was convicted of regicide and sentenced to be drawn and quartered. The punishment would take place in public. It was considered important that the public witness the punishment of those who had transgressed the law for the purposes of deterrence and to reinforce the power of the enforcer, the king.

Damiens' countenance was calm. His comment to Torcia's Congress was short: "The people want a spectacle. They want to be entertained. I will be that entertainment."

Damiens was taken to a public square in Rehna, where he was physically tortured to seek information about the crime and to be made ready for his execution. His punishment began with flesh being torn from his breast, arms, thighs, and calves with red-hot pincers, while in his right hand he held the knife he had used to commit the attempted assassination. Damien's body was burnt using sulphur, molten wax and lead, with boiling oil poured into his wounds. His cries were heard by all.

As ordered by Torcia's Congress, Damiens was drawn and quartered. Horses were harnessed to his arms and legs for his dismemberment. When his joints did not break as expected, the crowd grew impatient. They wanted to hear the bones crack and his final shrieks. Torcia's Congress ordered the executioner to have his aides finish the process by cutting Damiens' joints.

To the applause of the crowd, Damiens was dismembered. His trunk, apparently still living, was then burnt at the stake and his ashes thrown to the wind.[22] The people cheered!

Time Travel With Damiens - Ongoing.
Damiens Is The Same Man But Has Taken On A New Face and Form.

Damiens was born with power. He took over leadership of his country from his family. He governed and was accepted as a leader for many years. He had been born into a family wealthy from the exploration and development of Torcia's natural resources. He served in the military for three months as a gesture to show his dedication to his country. He flaunted his riches by building grand homes and establishing extensive land holdings.

Damiens was supported by other countries until unrest developed because he was seeking to extend his power throughout the world. People learnt of his activities to keep power by creating black lists of countries that disagreed with him and by murdering dissidents who did not agree with his country's political and economic system. People learnt of Damiens having waged wars against other countries to gain more territory.

People around the world watched his arrest, trial, and conviction on their televisions. The people were oblivious to his cries of injustice when he was arrested, during his trial, and at his execution. They listened to the taunting voices of his executioners. People heard the political voices that promoted and sanctioned his execution and were told he had committed crimes against humanity and killed his fellow citizens for power and money. They were told

---

22 This part of the vignette was inspired by writings of Michel Foucault in his works about discipline and punishment and the history of the assassination attempt on Louis XV in France by the assailant Damiens.

Damiens was a threat to the world because he was holding weapons of mass destruction. Torcian people said that they had heard the message before and once again, because Torcia´s National television had broadcast the news, they believed it was true.

The people grew impatient and did not wait to determine what weapons, if any, he held. They were satisfied Damiens was a threat to society and he was sentenced to be hanged.

Damiens´ countenance was calm. His final comment to the media before he was hanged was: "The people want a spectacle. They want to be entertained. I will be that entertainment."

Time Travel With Damiens - Cyberspace.
Damiens Is The Same Man But Has Again Taken On A New Face And Form.

Damiens is a photographer who had taken photographs of the people of Torcia. His photographs were intended to capture the reality of all, races, ages and classes of people in Torcia, the rich, the poor, the beautiful, and the deformed. He distributed his photographs on social network sites around the world.

Damiens was arrested for sex offences and treason. His arrest caused an outrage across the world. Internet portals sent information and blogs called for his immediate release. People watched his arrest and bail hearing on television and heard the strict conditions he was required to make to ensure he would not escape the jurisdiction where he was being held.

The plot was complicated; people could not decide if Damiens was a good man, a criminal, or perhaps both.

The woman, Luscious Lorna, entered Damiens´ room. She went straight to his bathroom where Damiens had just taken a shower. He wondered if Luscious Lorna was a staff member of the hotel. He wondered if she was a prostitute or spy sent to frame him.

There was also a man or woman in the shadows beside Damiens´ computer looking at Daniens´ computer files.

"Why are you in my hotel room, Damiens enquired?"

Luscious Lorna replied, "I came in to …"

Damiens cut her off. "Who are you"? You want something from me, don't you…?

I want to know what you want from me.

What is that person doing with my computer? What are you looking for"?

Luscious Lorna moved closer. The man or woman in the shadows beside his computer was moving or removing, creating or deleting computer files. Luscious Lorna moved even closer to Damiens. She opened her robe and her body hid the man or woman beside the computer.

Damiens' next encounter with Luscious Lorna and the person beside the computer was to see their names on the indictment against him for sexual assault and treason.

Torcia State Justice Department disclosed that it has two witnesses, Luscious Lorna and X. Both will be called as State witnesses at Damiens' trial. X has claimed witness protection by the State and his or her name, therefore, cannot be disclosed.

Damiens was been brought to trial on the charges of sexual assault and treason[23].

Damiens' countenance was calm. His comment to the media before trial was:

"The people want a spectacle. They want to be entertained. Again, I will be that entertainment."

The Judgement Game:

You have been given only a small amount of information about Luscious Lorna and X. You are asked to use your imagination and knowledge of the politics and news events in the country where you lived prior to becoming a citizen of Torcia in order to create your own story about what Luscious Lorna and X were doing in Damiens' room?

---

23 Treason: betrayal of one's own country by waging war against it or by consciously or purposely acting to aid its enemies.

Writing the Story

1) Who was Luscious Lorna?

_____

_____

_____

2) What did Luscious Lorna want from Damiens?

_____

_____

_____

3) Who is X?

_____

_____

_____

4) What did X want from Damiens?

_____

_____

_____

5) Was Damiens waging war against his country, Torcia, or was he consciously or purposely acting to aid its enemies. Why might Torcia want to allege that Damiens was guilty of treason?

_____

_____

_____

The Judgement Game: Your Decision

1) In the first part of the vignette, "Time Travel With Damiens Commences" was Damiens an:

Offender ____

Victim ____

Both ___

2) In the second part of the vignette, "Time Travel With Damiens: Ongoing" was Damiens an:

Offender ___

Victim ___

Both ___

3) In the last part of the vignette, " Time Travel With Damiens: Cyberspace," was Damiens an:

Offender ___

Victim ___

Both ___

4) How will Damiens be punished if he is found guilty of the two charges in Time Travel With Damiens: Cyberspace?

Hanging ___

Incarceration ___

Banishment from Torcia ___

Some Other Form of Punishment?

_____

_____

_____

5) Is this the end of "Time Travel With Damiens"?

Yes [ ]   No [ ]

Why or Why Not?

_____

_____

_____

6) Does the vignette "Time Travel With Damiens" provide a message about entertainment of Torcian people?

_____

_____

_____

7) Does the vignette "Time Travel With Damiens" provide a message about punishment?

_____

_____

_____

8) What role do the people of Torcia play in the vignette "Time Travel With Damiens"?

_____

_____

_____

Self-Assessment

You have the opportunity to provide a self-assessment after reading the vignettes in "Defining the Issues."

    Indicate how many points* you give yourself for:

    1) Recognition of issues raised in the chapter.   ____

    2) Suggestions and comments you made.   ____

    3) Your role as a decision maker.   ____

    TOTAL: ____

*You can give yourself 0 (lowest) to 5 (highest) points.

This is a game. Remember there are no right or wrong answers.

CHAPTER 11:
A NEW WAY

* * *

A PARABLE: THE WAYS OF THE PAST

We must pay for the wrongs we have done to others. Particular consideration should be given to those whose lands we invaded, the people who were here before us. We took from them their culture, their self-respect, and their gods. We gave them horses, liquor, guns, and shiny baubles. We gave them our religion, our political system, and our form of education. We gave them our justice system. We judged them and gave them homes in our prisons.

When we released them from prison, we told them to look after themselves. They said, "No, we can't."

We said, "Yes, you must!"

Some of them were blinded by the past and wanted to stay in their secure prison cells. They were not able to escape the comfort of recidivism. Others left their prison cells to integrate with their communities and to move forward with a new life.

Torcia´s justice system remained the same.

We gave them back their lands. They bought shiny new pickup trucks with the money they received and then abandoned the trucks outside the prefabs we had also given them.

The justice system is the same.

Torcian people have spoken. They say:

"We want something different"!

What does Torcia want?

LOOKING FOR A NEW WAY

Does Torcia want to build a criminal justice system that reflects community conscientiousness and equality, or does it want to continue using a criminal justice system that follows an old model?

_____

_____

_____

Are the good things that can be adopted from the old model?

_____

_____

_____

What should be discarded from the old model?

_____

_____

_____

Does Torcia want to shift its sentencing model from incarceration to integration and provide people an opportunity to live outside prison walls?

_____

_____

_____

Does Torcia want a system of restorative justice that recognizes the needs of victims and offenders?

_____

_____

_____

Does Torcia´s criminal justice system need to respond to the public?

_____

_____

_____

Do television programmes provide accurate information about the criminal justice system?

_____

_____

_____

Are televised legal trials a form of entertainment for the people in Torcia or do they provide important information about crime or both?

_____

_____

_____

Does Torcia need to take its criminal justice system back from the professionals trained to write the laws, interpret the laws, and enforce the laws?

_____

_____

_____

Provide your comments about your role as a citizen of Torcia in shaping the criminal justice system.

_____

_____

_____

What should Torcia do with its immoral citizens, i.e. those who refuse to adhere to Torcia's laws?

_____

_____

_____

Will there always be a place for prisons in Torcia?

_____

_____

_____

Highlights from Torcia National News!
CYBER-CRIME ON THE RISE
VIOLENCE AGAINST WOMEN
THREE STAFF- TWO PRISONERS INJURED IN RIOT
MOTHER'S MARCH AGAINST GANG VIOLENCE
LATEST CRIME STATISTICS
WAR AGAINST DRUGS
PRISON BREAK
HATE CRIMES SPIKE AFTER BILL PASSES
DRUG BUST TARGETS REDA MAFIA
LATEST CRIME STATISTICS
MISSING!
DISTRACTION BURGLARY
VIOLENCE AGAINST ELDERS
Do news broadcasts play an important role in providing information to Torcia's people?
YES [ ] NO [ ]

What Punishment Have You Decided to use?
The Old Model
Yes [ ]
No [ ]

194

or

A New Way?

Yes ☐

No ☐

or

A Little Bit of Both.

Yes ☐

No ☐

DID YOU WIN THE JUDGEMENT GAME?

You Need 100 Points to win the game.
Ten points are awarded for each answer where you check "Yes".

I read the book.   Yes ☐ No ☐

I completed the questions.   Yes ☐ No ☐

I made the decisions requested of me.   Yes ☐ No ☐

I thought about why the offenders
breached the laws.   Yes ☐ No ☐

I thought about definitions of
victim and offender.   Yes ☐ No ☐

I learnt something about
crime and punishment.   Yes ☐ No ☐

I learnt something about justice.   Yes ☐ No ☐

I am not able to say
"one sentence fits all".   Yes ☐ No ☐

I learnt that all offenders were once
little boys and little girls.   Yes ☐ No ☐

I enjoyed the game.   Yes ☐ No ☐

YOUR POINTS ___
DID YOU WIN THE JUDGEMENT GAME? ___

MYSTERY QUESTION: What is the most serious crime in *The Judgement Game?* _____
(The book title provides the clue)

SELF ASSESSMENT- Maximum of 150 points
YOUR POINTS ___
HOW DID YOU DO? ___/150

ANNEX A: OUTLINE OF SENTENCING PRINCIPLES FOR THE JUDGEMENT GAME[24]

RETRIBUTION:

The need to ensure the offender is adequately punished for the offence. The offender's sentence should be proportionate to the seriousness of the offence and the degree of responsibility of the offender.

DETERRENCE:

Punishment to warn the offender and other people of the consequences of criminal behavior.

General Deterrence: The offender is punished in order to deter other people from committing similar offences.

Specific Deterrence: Punishment used to deter the individual offender from committing similar offences in the future.

REHABILITATION:

This concept means to restore the offender to a useful and a non-criminal way of life often through the use of therapy and education. One of the objectives of this principle is to address the underlying cause/s of the offender's criminal behaviour. The concept of rehabilitation assumes that people are not inherently criminal and can be restored to a useful life in which they can benefit themselves and society. One goal of rehabilitation is to prevent habitual offences or recidivism.

---

24 Many books have been written about sentencing and sentencing principles. This brief outline of concepts is to provide the reader with a general understanding of the principles to assist with responses to questions asked in *The Judgement Game.*

RESTORATIVE JUSTICE:

Restorative justice or reparative justice seeks to focus on the needs of victims and offenders, as well as involving the community. The offender is encouraged to accept responsibility for his or her offence and often to repair the harm caused by the offence. Examples or repairing harm include: returning stolen items, providing services to the community, and sending letters of apology to the victim.

ANNEX B: EXTRACTS FROM TORCIAN LAW

The Annex sets out Torcia's laws: These laws are the only laws you need to play the game. Torcia does not provide you with all of Torcia´s laws, only what you need to play *The Judgement Game.*

Force of Law: This is law *only* in Torcia and to be used exclusively for your decisions in *The Judgement Game.* These laws have no force and effect anywhere except Torcia and in this book.

Returning Justice to the People: You do not need to be a lawyer or judge to play *The Judgement Game.* They too can play but must remember this is a work of fiction and there are no right or wrong answers. The book is about returning justice to the people. Offenders and the laws are fictitious and created only to encourage the reader to provide his or her ideas about the justice system of Torcia.

Sentencing Concepts in *The Judgement Game:* Penalties are specified in the text or, where not specified, range from Absolute Discharge, Conditional Discharge, Fines, Probation, or Incarceration from one day to life imprisonment. Capital punishment is not a punishment in Torcia. Should a reader believe that penalty should be available he or she has the right to make the suggestion in his or her comments. You are self-taught and your knowledge and opinions about sentencing concepts are valued and accepted.

* Readers are asked to recognise the expertise of those who work with the law in Torcia and other countries: the legislators, lawyers, legal academics, the judiciary, and people dealing with sentencing, corrections and penal policies.*

*Throughout *The Judgement Game,* wherever the plural is used it shall be construed as including the singular or vice versa, and the masculine shall be construed as including the feminine or a body corporate, all as the gender, number, or context may require. *

ASSAULT:

When a person employs force against another person that is not momentary or fleeting, or causes the other person to believe that force will be used against him that is not momentary or fleeting.

ASSAULT CAUSING BODILY HARM:

An assault, as defined by Torcian law, that causes bodily harm to a person.

ASSAULT OF PARTNER:

(1) Where a person

(a) intentionally uses force against a partner that is not momentary and fleeting;

(b) purposely causes a partner to believe that force that is not momentary and fleeting will be used against him.

(2) For this provision, partner means: a spouse, former spouse, person with whom he has a child, person that he is dating or with whom he has a serious physical relationship, whether that person is of the opposite or the same sex.

(3) An offender found guilty of assault of a partner is liable to a minimum period of imprisonment of three months and a maximum penalty of ten years.

BODILY HARM:

Any harm or injury to a person that is not momentary or fleeting.

CAUSING DEATH BY CRIMINAL NEGLIGENCE WHEN OPERATING A MOTOR VEHICLE:

Where a Torcian citizen, while operating a motor vehicle, causes death to another person by his negligence or inability to operate the motor vehicle, the offender is liable to a minimum period of imprisonment of ten years and a maximum penalty of life imprisonment.

CONSENT:
When the person has permission to do something.

CONTROL:
When the person has power over or directs
    (a) the act and how it will be accomplished, or
    (b) the place where an offence occurs.

CRIMINAL ENDANGERMENT:
When a person has knowledge and understanding of his actions, acts in a manner that causes significant risk to another person of death or serious bodily harm or fails to act in a manner that causes significant risk to another person of death or serious bodily harm.

CRIMINAL NEGLIGENCE:
Where a person has a duty to act to ensure the safety and well-being of another person or persons and fails to exercise that duty, or is careless or reckless in exercising that duty.

DEFENCE OF ENTRAPMENT:
There is no substantive defence of entrapment in Torcia for drug offences.

DUTY:
A legal responsibility to act in a prescribed manner.

IMPORTING HEROIN:
Torcia imposes a mandatory sentence of imprisonment for importing heroin. The offence has a minimum period of imprisonment of five years and a maximum penalty of life imprisonment; the sentence to be based on the quantity of heroin imported.

KNOWLEDGE:
To be aware of a fact or information.

MANSLAUGHTER:
The killing, of one person by another person without premeditation or deliberation.

MURDER:
The unlawful premeditated killing of one person by another person.

NO-CONTACT ORDER:
An order prohibiting one person from interfering with another person.

PARTY TO AN OFFENCE:
A person is a party to an offence where he:
(1) actually commits the offence; or
(2) does or omits to do anything for the purpose of helping another person commit the offence.

POSSESSION (Torcia Drug Laws)
(1) A person is in possession of an item where he:
(a) has the item in his actual possession; or
(b) has the item in the custody of another person, or
(c) has the item in a place over which he has control.

(2) Where one person, with the knowledge of others, has an item in his possession, Torcian law directs that the item is in the possession of all.

RECKLESS DRIVING:
When a person drives a motor vehicle without regard for the safety and well-being of other people.

SELF-DEFENCE PROVISION:
When a person is assaulted and fears death or injury, without having provoked the assault, the person may repel the assault against him with reasonable force to defend himself.

SENTENCING CONCEPTS:
Penalties are specified in the text or, where not specified, range from Absolute Discharge, Conditional Discharge, Fines, Probation, or Incarceration from one day to life imprisonment. Capital punishment is not a punishment in Torcia. Should a reader believe that penalty should be available he or she has the right to make the suggestion in his or her comments. You are self-taught and your knowledge and opinions about the sentencing concepts are valued and accepted.

STALKING:
Torcia defines stalking as any of the following acts:
(1) watching a person or following a person;
(2) taking steps to contact a person in any way, including by telephone, mail, using photography or by any form of electronic communication;
(3) intimidating, harassing or any way threatening a person.
Stalking is punishable with a maximum period of imprisonment of ten years. There is no minimum penalty.

TRAFFICKING:
Passing goods or items from one person to another person.

TREASON:
The betrayal of one's country by acting with intent to assist its enemies.

UTTERING A DEATH THREAT:
A person who, in any way, conveys or utters a threat to cause death or bodily harm to another person.

DEDICATION

Dedicated to my parents and grandparents.

CPSIA information can be obtained at www.ICGtesting.com
Printed in the USA
LVOW01s0933091113

360636LV00032B/2368/P

9 781481 945912